Elizabeth R. Charles

Against the Stream

Vol. I

Elizabeth R. Charles

Against the Stream
Vol. I

ISBN/EAN: 9783337193584

Printed in Europe, USA, Canada, Australia, Japan

Cover: Foto ©Andreas Hilbeck / pixelio.de

More available books at **www.hansebooks.com**

AGAINST THE STREAM

—

VOL I.

AGAINST THE STREAM

The Story of an Heroic Age in England

BY THE AUTHOR OF

"THE SCHONBERG-COTTA FAMILY"

IN THREE VOLS.—I.

STRAHAN & CO.
56, LUDGATE HILL, LONDON
1873

LONDON ·
PRINTED BY VIRTUE AND CO
CITY ROAD.

CHAPTER I.

NO one who has not tried can imagine what a pleasant thing it is to be, undeniably and consciously, an old woman.

I mean, of course, literally, not symbolically.

To have the whole landscape of life behind you, and below you. To see, now and then, indications through the mists and shadows, why the path wound here through barren, empty wastes, and there through thorny thickets; in one place scaled recklessly the perilous rocky steep, in another crept in weary windings along monotonous slopes it had seemed easier to

VOL. I.   B

clear at a bound; or why, just there, it
broke off in a sudden chasm, which at the
time threatened to end its meaning and
waste its work altogether. To catch some
explanatory hints of a training of eye and
nerve for higher work hereafter; some
illuminated glimpses of fellow-travellers,
to be succoured just at that perplexing
turn, and nowhere else. To have the long
uphill all but over, and to find " the up-
land slopes of duty " all but merging in
the " table-land of glory," as they do, not
for the exceptional hero only, but for all
who follow the footprints of the Master's
feet, if the Master's words are true; if
heroism means, as He showed, not exceptional achievement, but self-surrendering
obedience; and glory, as He is showing
now, not some vague repetition of earthly
pomps with a larger than earthly audience,
but the expansion and illumination of every
faculty, in a life fuller than the intensest

life below, for a service higher because nearer Him.

To watch such explanatory broken lights stealing over the past that reaches back so far;—to catch the dawn of unbroken, satisfying light on the future, now so near. Rest here, in the acquiescence in powers enfeebled, unequal to fresh enterprise, that have done their work and can undertake no more, save such stray quiet kindnesses as may come to us demanding to be done; rest here, in the hope of powers renewed, so that their exercise shall become once more a joy, such as it was to move or breathe in childhood.

A little faint insight through the learning and unlearning of the years,—through their tenderer tolerance, and larger judgments, into the patience of Him who has been teaching and long-suffering through the ages. A strong and ever-growing trust, through some discords resolved, and some despairs clashed into hopes; through some misunderstood things explained, and some wrongs righted or turned into sacred instruments of martyrdom, through much forgiven and something overcome—in the purpose of Him "who willeth not that any should perish," not because sin is a mere passing disease of the childhood of humanity, or a mere passing discord of the harmonies of the universe, but because "He willeth that all men should repent." A bright and ever brightening hope in a heaven which shall be the seed-plot of many heavens, through that Death which is the seed of infinite life.

To find the "great multitude no man can number," the "majority" to which we go, no longer an overwhelming dazzle of supernatural light, a crowd of unknown, unindividualised angelic faces, but the blessed company where the dearest eyes wonder and smile, and the most familiar voices are heard, in that speech at once so tender and so high we know not what better to call it than song.

These things are worth waiting for, worth growing old for, worth having this world emptied for.

Can I say that?

Not always; not most healthily, I think, in moments of ecstatic foreseeing, but in those moments more frequent, when it is given me, in some simple ways, to fill up the measure of their service who have gone before, and so to feel that, after all, this world is indeed not empty to me, though my best have gone on out of sight.

So vividly they stand before me, those old times, now that the morning mists and the noon-day haze are over, and the mists of night have scarcely come; so clearly do the old voices sound back to me in the quiet, especially from the earliest days, and so different is the world whence they come from this around me now, that I feel attracted to sit down and picture them, with just as little effort as if I were not making pictures at all, but simply tracing outlines of the reflections on a series of mirrors, and transforming them thus, by some magic, into a series of stained-glass windows.

So it seems to me.

But then, of course, I always see the clear living mirror behind my outlines; and how far the stained glass represents it to others I cannot know.

It is worth while to do it, for myself at least, for I have lived through one of our country's heroic ages, and, as it seems to me, have seen some of the heroes not very far off.

And, in looking back over my life, if there are any principles which have been its joy and strength, and which I could wish to see more the joy and strength of others, they are these.

Christianity is to me, and ever has

been since I learned to live by it, not so much a fresh mystery, as a revelation of mysteries—a "mystery shown;" not a clouding, but an unveiling; not a new riddle, whose glory is that being the divinest it is the deepest, but a solution of many riddles, although indeed not yet of all.

The world and its great history are full of darkness; society and our own little histories are full of darkness, and much of this Christianity has left unconquered and un-explained.

But at the heart and centre of all is not darkness, but light; not only a mind in-finite and incomprehensible, but a heart that loves and speaks; not a subtle setter-forth of riddles which humanity has to solve at its peril, or perish, but a patient teacher of babes, to whom His human creatures are dear; not an inexorable medical examiner testing candidates for appointments, but the

Physician healing the sick; not the Sphinx, but the Word.

Truth obvious indeed, and at the root of all Christian theology (is not the absence of it practically Atheism?), yet from which it seems to me most Christian theologies are for ever departing into labyrinths of our own making, and ever needing to be recalled.

And flowing from this is another principle, which has strengthened me to live and hope. The light, and not the darkness, is meant to conquer, in individuals, as in the whole. Human character is not immutable, like the instincts of animals, but corrigible and perfectible;—perfectible in the best to the end, corrigible in the worst to the end;—capable of radical change, capable of infinite growth.

Again, truth most obvious, if Christianity is true; yet one which in the apparent fixedness of character in all men after early youth, and the apparent invincibility of small faults in good men, in wrong from others, in struggles with myself, I, at least, have not found it easy to hold; which, indeed, I should have found it impossible to hold, but for constant recurrence to that first great truth which is its source.

Faith in God, unbounded; and, for that reason, hope for men unbounded also.

Are these things so easy to hold in a world where the chaos of a French revolution can whirl on for a century without evolving a creation?—where the Church of land after land, and age after age, has succeeded too often in silencing its noblest men?—where a Las Casas originated the slave-trade, and the abolition of slavery has not at all events resulted in a planter's Paradise of grateful industrious labourers?—where a century of philanthropic efforts leaves our English legislation powerless to lift off the accumulating weight of pauperism, and a millennium of Christianity

leaves English Christians powerless to stem
the increasing flood of intemperance?—
where in our own little worlds all of us
have seen the race not always won by the
swift, nor the battle by the brave?

Do we not need in such a world a faith in
God, which, whatever is doubtful and what-
ever is dark, leaves it not doubtful that "in
Him is no darkness at all?"

Do we not need a hope for man that has
its root deeper than in any man, or in any
history, even in Him who loving most has
suffered most; Who "underwent and over-
came;" Whose life was serving, Whose
victory was in being vanquished, Whose
reigning is serving, Whose reward for the
service of His own is to serve better, Whose
work in the midst of the throne is the old
familiar shepherd's work of "leading" and
feeding, Whose triumph in the day of His
joy will be to "gird himself, and come
forth, and serve?"

And this leads me to the third living principle of my life;—belief in a heaven which is not a contradiction, but a completion of true Christian life below; in a Master whose promise is, not a rewarding of seventy years of toil by an eternity of luxurious repose; nor an avenging of seventy years of abasement by an eternity of exaltation; nor a compensation for seventy years of service and suffering by an eternity of triumphal pomp and regal state; but a training by the numbered years of imperfect work here for an eternity of blessed work, unhindered and unwearied; by seventy years of gradual deliverance from the bondage of self, not for an eternity of the gratification of self, intellectual or spiritual, but for an eternity of the only liberty worth having, the Liberty, not of the Rights of independent atoms, but of the Duties of a mutually dependent brotherhood, in the presence of the Father whom

all obey, and on whom all depend; the
glorious Liberty of Love, the necessity of
whose nature, like His who is its source and
end, is to give, and in giving, before and in
all its gifts, to give itself, giving and receiving in that endless interchange which
ensures growth, and which only is worthy
to be called life.

A belief I have found not without practical importance: since earnests and fore-
tastes of our promised inheritance are sure
to be coveted by the way, and it makes not
a little difference to our practical life
whether we consider the truest symbol and
foretaste of heaven to be the contemplation
of toiling cities from suburban paradises, or
the succouring and serving the poorest creature toiling in those city streets.

If I have had any power in my life to
"lift up hands that hang down," to revive
now and then hope for humanity in some
veterans (to whom I have been as a child),

worn-out with the disappointments of many
victories which have failed to accomplish all
they seemed to promise; or, in some fallen
creatures, worn-out with the despair of
many defeats, it is to such simple and
obvious principles as these that I owe it.

And yet how vain to think we know the
springs of the influences which have
moulded us, or through which we have
acted on others; so subtle are they, so
simple, so subtly combined, so finely distinct!

Deeper even than its deepest principles is
our religion, rooted not in a principle, but in
the Person we adore; and, since the divine
history is ever deeper and wider than all
the theologies and philosophies drawn from
it, to me, doubtless, as to all, from the
wisest to the simplest, all true power to
live, or to help to live, has come from Him
Who, while in Himself revealing the Father,
understood and saved the "sinner" who

washed His feet, hoped in and saved the disciple who denied Him, loved and saved the Pharisee who "persecuted Him," Whose presence makes heaven, and must make a heaven like Himself.

We may review or analyze our life into principles, as we analyze our food into alkalies, salts, and acids; but no chemical combination of alkalies, salts, and acids yet invented will keep us alive.

Principles must, after all, be rooted in affections: life can only be nourished by life.

CHAPTER II.

" Fretted by sallies of his mother's kisses,
  With light upon him from his father's eyes."

SUCH Recollections of early childhood with me are all too soon broken in upon.

Yet to me also the world began with Paradise. I can dimly recall such a zone of tenderest sunlight, such a sense of being watched and delighted in, brooded and purred over, and played with; such a golden time of kisses and coaxings, and tender foldings up at night, and laughing wakings up in the morning.

And then, succeeding it, a time of silence and darkness and cold; of being hushed and kept quiet because Something which had made the sunshine of the home was gone, and Something else which needed that lost sunshine more than any had come, and must be cherished and watched and kept alive with such artificial warmth as the world can make for motherless babes,— leaving at the moment little warmth and light to spare anywhere for me.

A dark confused chaotic time, "without form, and void;" in looking back, I can scarcely tell whether it lasted days, or months, or years; a time when God had made for me no lights, greater or lesser, to divide the light from the darkness.

So my first associations with my brother, my own brother Piers, who was afterwards the life of my life, were rather of something subtracted than something added, rather of a great loss, than the great gift he was.

I think we shall find it thus with many of our best gifts, often.

After this comes first into my recollection

a pervading and overshadowing memory of Clothes.

Before, it was like being a bird or a flower. But connected with that dark chaotic time comes a sense of being in a state of existence where one had always to carry about Things to be taken care of, which one was in some vague and uneasy way identified with and responsible for, and which the people in the nursery who loved one most, felt to be in some sense of more importance than oneself, and yet the very nature of which appeared to be that the influences which were pleasant to their wearer were pernicious to them.

It was, I suppose, the form in which my spirit had to struggle into the consciouness of matter,

> " Obstinate questionings,
> Blank misgivings of a creature
> Moving about in worlds not realised."

How many of the lessons incident to the "shades of the prison-house" came to me

through my Clothes!—through that portion
of the material world which was to me so
essentially part of the "Not Me," and was
evidently regarded by those around me as
an integral portion of the "Me!"

I can remember now the delighted sense
of freedom with which, one Sunday afternoon, I had crept, unnoticed, out of the
garden door, with my faithful companion,
our great black Newfoundland dog, Pluto,
up the green hill outside the garden wall to
the edge of the brook beyond, and was
enjoying at once the joys of liberty and of
tyranny in making him plunge into the
water and fetch me a stick, as I had seen
my father do. I remember now the half-
remonstrant, the half-condescending way in
which the grand creature yielded to my
little imperiousness, and then, landing his
freight, shook himself in a storm of sparkling drops over me and my new frock.

And I also remember a certain calm

philosophical interest (which ought in any
consistent biography to have presaged a
genius for scientific investigation) where-
with I was observing that the drops did not
penetrate my crape, but lay on it, round and
sparkling,—when nurse burst upon us with
baby in her arms and a wail on her lips.

"Bless the maid ! what will she be after
next? Miss Bride, Miss Bride, you contrary child, how can you be so unfeeling as
to forget your new crape, and your blessed
mother, and Sunday, and everything, and
romp about like a beggar's brat with that
great brute of a dog?"

A speech which left me in such a bewilderment of images and injustices that I
was too perplexed to cry or to defend
myself, until the dog, his affections getting
the better of his tact, shook himself in a
rapture of welcome over baby and nurse,
and thereby drew on himself a blow which
sent him away whining in his inarticulate

way; whilst I, tearfully protesting that Pluto was not a brute nor I a brat, and that I had not forgotten Sunday, for father had only just given me my Sunday gingerbread, was dragged down the steps of the dear old garden, from terrace to terrace, whining in my half-articulate way.

And I also remember to this day my father standing at the door of the summer parlour, which opened on the garden, welcoming me with open arms, caressing and comforting me, and saying that "Clothes did not matter at all, if I would only be his own dear little Bride, and not cry."

But Clothes did matter, as I knew too well in my feminine experience, and as nurse protested, "How should master know about Clothes, poor dear soul, who had neither to make nor to mend, nor to starch nor to iron? Men, the wisest of them, always talked as if clothes grew upon children like fur upon kittens."

They mattered, indeed, so much to me, that I had never any difficulty at all in receiving the narrative of Genesis connecting Clothes with the fall rather than the creation of man, as a most rational explanation of the nature of things, being already quite convinced from my own history that they could never have been originally intended as essentials in any beneficent scheme of the universe.

Only, Piers and I used in after years frequently to lament that the primitive institution of skins had not been adhered to.

Also, I suspect, Clothes had much to do with that next step which made so great a change in our lives.

I have little doubt it was a sense of his incapacity for contending with the difficulties springing, not from the characters of his children, but from their Clothes, feminine and infantine, with all the feminine care and attendance incident thereunto, that induced my father to place at the head of his house the discreet and sober-minded gentle-woman who became our stepmother; clothes, I mean, in the larger sense,—conventionalities, customs, proprieties.

The reign of Clothes certainly did not cease with my stepmother. Only the signification of the word extended. Conventionalities, customs, proprieties, all the ritual of life, these were her standard measures, her household gods, her sacred Scriptures, or at least her tradition of the elders, which brought them down to practice; her Talmud if not her Pentateuch. With most of us, I suppose, our practical commentaries are unwritten.

On the Upper Olympus, doubtless, with her as with others, sate enthroned the serene far-off orthodox divinities, but by the hearth were acknowledged two presiding powers, one deprecated as the root of mischief, and the other honoured with daily incense and libation. Her evil genius was Enthusiasm; her protecting divinity, Moderation.

To understand the Bible or anything properly, she would have considered that every text should be underlined with "Let everything be done decently and in order," and, "Let your moderation be known unto all men."

With her, sin was doing anything too vehemently; heresy, believing anything too intensely; justice between contending parties was thinking every one equally wrong; charity, thinking every one equally right; the Christian warfare an armed neutrality; truth, the residuum after the extraction of all extreme opinions; paradise, the place where all exaggerated ideas and characters are either absent or kept quiet.

At least such was the impression she made on me in the exaggerations of my childish imagination; for hers was a mode-

ration which always tempted me into extremes, and it was only later that I learned
to be just to her. She was as kind as any
one can be without sympathy, as just as
any one can be without imagination. She
adhered as faithfully to the golden rule,
"As ye would that men should do to you,
do ye also to them," as any one can do who
has no conception of the differences between
men, between the "they" and the "you,"
no idea of the patient study of circumstance
and character which the true fulfilling of
the precept involves.

In later years, moreover, we grew to
understand each other better; as she and
I both learned, I trust, something from each
other, and more from life.

In earlier years, I can see now, if not the
good she did me, at least something of the
evils from which she kept me.

It is good for us all to have some ice
early in our lives. It makes the air fresher,

and restrains the enthusiasm which is meant to enrich the summers and middle levels with living waters and live-giving soil, from overflowing too early in the spring-time on the higher levels, and so evaporating in mists of sentiment, or being lost in marshes of vague good intention.

Much fond and foolish talk there was, no doubt, in the nursery, when it was announced that Mr. Danescombe, my father, was about to marry Miss Euphrasia Weston.

Faltering exhortations were addressed to me by nurse as to the duties of our new relationship to the good lady who was coming to be our "new mother," congratulations whose compassionate tones made me interpret them into condolences. For children, like dogs, read speech as if it were music, by tones rather than by words.

The only words of her exhortations which made any impressions on me were those

terrible promises of a "new mother." To
me they were what to a devout Jew might
have been the promise of a "new god."

In those days the French words, vul-
garised by bad nursery pronunciation into
papa and mamma, which would be so intolerable if they were not hallowed to two or
three generations by the lispings of baby
lips, had not yet been introduced into
England, or at least had not penetrated
to our social level in our little country
town. There was, therefore, no convenient
intermediate conventional term, expressive
rather of position than relationship.

And the sacred name, mother, was not,
in my Protestant childhood, distributed in
the liberal manner since the fashion among
any benevolent ladies who undertake the
charge of young girls, good or naughty.
In those days women only became mothers
through a mother's anguish and joy.

To me "mother" meant one only incom-

parable love, one only irreparable loss ; love
which had loved *me*, me as I was, not any
goodness or beauty in me, not my clothes,
nor my behaviour, but me, her little, helpless, longing, clinging Bride ; loss which had
left my childhood, consciously or unconsciously, one long empty craving, " feeling
after if haply I might find" wings to brood
over me, arms to fold me like hers.

And now nurse seemed to expect me
to transfer that dear lost name in this easy
way to an unknown quantity, as if it meant
nothing, like a nonsense nursery rhyme ; as
if life meant nothing but a " make-believe"
play with dolls !

I could not have done so even to an old
doll. Yet to remonstrate with any one
who could have had the want of perception
to propose such a thing was, I instinctively
felt, as useless as trying to explain the
mysteries of property to Pluto.

I cried myself to sleep silently that night,

in one of those unutterable agonies of childhood.   Happily childish agonies do not
drive sleep away !

And the next morning I awoke and
began my vain tears again, but made no
moan or complaint, until nurse finding I
did not get on with my bread and milk,
began one of her half-caressing, half-queru-
lous remonstrances.

"What ails the child ? Miss Bride, you
are getting quite beyond poor old nurse.
And so no doubt others have thought.
May-be the new lady will manage better."

Then I broke out into one gasping sob,
and said, "Must I call the new lady
Mother ?"

"Sure enough, child, sure enough ! what
would poor dear master say ?"

"Did father say that ?"

"Who would make so bold as to ask
him ? Never mind, poor lamb, never mind;
what's the name ? The *name's* nothing."

To me the name was unutterably much. But I was consoled by perceiving that it was plain nurse had no sentence on the matter from my father ; and I secretly resolved to ask him myself.

To me the name was everything. To use it falsely was, I felt in some dim way, to bring a lie into my life, or rather to sap all significance out of the words false-hood and truth, to make all language, all sacred words and names lose their distinc-tive meaning and become mere interchange-able hollownesses. That is to say, this is what I now know my instinctive revulsion meant.

The very next time that I sate on my father's knee, and could get my face well hidden on his breast, with desperate cou-rage I began—

"Must I call her Mother ?"

His hands trembled as they stroked my hair, and his lips as they kissed me, and I

could hear that his voice was half choked as
he said—

" Who, little Bride?   What does my
darling mean ?"

"The new lady," I said, without lifting
my head.

He put me down, and paced hastily up
and down the room ; and then he said, in
what seemed to me a very cold and absent
voice, " I will ask her."

But then again he suddenly seized me
in his arms and pressed me to his heart, and
I felt his tears as he said—

" Little Bride, my darling little Bride,
you are not afraid of me ?   I am only bringing some one home to take care of you and
baby."

And so he fully believed, my poor father.
Bewildered by the advice of some and the
gossip of others, and the well-meant queru-
lousness of nurse, and the various feminine
and infantine incomprehensibilities of baby

and of me, he was bringing home this sage
and sober-minded new lady who talked
good English, which nurse did not, and
was a good economist, which he was not,
to preside over his household, his children,
and himself, to provide us with costumes
and catechisms, with clothes, intellectual,
moral, and material.

I am not describing typical relationships
or characters. Relationships and characters
are not to be so easily classified into types.
Second marriages are as different as first
marriages, and stepmothers as different as
mothers or mothers-in-law. But our country
town was not a normal community, nor was
mine a normal life. And this was my
experience.

The next day my father kissed me very
tenderly when I went to bed, and said
gravely—

"Miss Weston does not wish my little
Bride to call her anything that is not

strictly correct. You may call her Mrs.
Danescombe. She would like it."

I felt so relieved, and so grateful to the
new lady for the relief, I could almost have
welcomed her. I suppose a dim hope came
to me that she would after all understand
me.

A week after that my father went away
for a day or two. In those days wedding
journeys had not been introduced. He was
married in the neighbouring town where
Miss Euphrasia was staying, and the next
day he brought her home, and we were
summoned to greet her.

She stooped down graciously and gave
me her cheek to kiss; and she spoke in a
high-pitched caressing tone, supposed to
suit the infantine taste, to Piers, and made
a movement as if she would have taken
him in her arms and kissed him. But
she seemed to find her dress a little in the
way. She wore a drooping large-brimmed

hat with a feather, and ruffles and lappets and laces in various places, and I believe she felt shy with the child, which he with a child's instinct of course perceived; and concluding she had no right or pos- session in him, he turned from her with a little pout, and a little quiver of the lips, to me.

I saw her colour rise a little, and I felt rather than saw a slight uneasy frown on my father's face. I knew that things were going wrong; and then all at once some- thing motherly seemed to wake up in my own heart (I do not know what else to call it), a dim feeling that I was not there to be taken care of, but to take care of other people, of Piers and father, and even in some sense of Mrs. Danescombe. And I folded my arms around my little brother, and stretched out his little hands and mine together towards her, and then I seemed to feel father's frown relax to a smile, and

in a moment we were both caught up and
half smothered in his arms, and enveloped
in a comprehensive embrace in which Mrs.
Danescombe was in some way involved.

Then afterwards father hastily left the
room, as if he had finished the reconciliation scene in a play, his sanguine nature
quite satisfied that all was going right ; and
Mrs. Danescombe, after bestowing a toy on
Piers, and a new London doll on me, was
quite content to leave Piers to my guardianship, while she smoothed herself down
before the small cut Venetian glass in the
oaken frame over the old high-carved
chimney-piece.

And I remember sitting in the window-
seat with my arms around Piers, altogether
grave and happy with that new feeling of
motherliness. We did not touch our toys,
but sate gravely conversing ; so that when
our father returned, cheerily rubbing his
hands, he looked a little disappointed to see

the new gifts neglected, and said to me half reproachfully—

"Does not my little Bride care for her beautiful new doll?"

How could I? I, who was feeling wise and matronly as if I were the mother of the human race, and had the world on my shoulders, himself included!

Besides, what strange ideas he must have about dolls! Was a new doll to be made acquaintance with and taken to one's heart in a moment?

However, I took up the doll, and began to behave to it with great politeness.

And Mrs. Danescombe drew near us, and made sundry efforts to "amuse" Piers by jerking the angular wooden puppet with which she had presented him, by means of internal strings, into various mountebank attitudes, which were intended to be funny.

I remember now the sense of grave wonder and pity with which I contemplated these futile attempts at entertainment, whilst Piers continued to gaze steadily into her face, with serious, undeluded eyes, evidently concluding that she was quite too old to play, and that the whole thing was a piece of very ineffective dramatic performance. I think the courteous complaisance with which little children receive our imbecile attempts to amuse them very remarkable; they who are never taken in, who are themselves actors of the first-class, by instinct, living in a perpetually varied drama as gloriously independent of vulgar necessities of scene-painting as an Athenian audience; they to whom any few feet square of earth where they can be let alone are an imperial amphitheatre, and two chairs a hippodrome, and a heap of chips a fortune of theatrical properties.

Piers, I am sure, took in the whole futility and absurdity of the situation; but he also understood that the new lady meant

well, and like the little king he was, from
time to time he vouchsafed her the patronage
of a smile, and even condescended to imitate
her movements with the puppet.

Little king that he was! My little king
whom I would serve with all I was and had,
and guard and cherish, and pet and honour,
and keep the world warm for; and be his
interpreter, his queen, his slave!

That night I asked nurse if I might say
my prayers beside baby's crib, instead of at
her knee. The wonderful birds and flowers
on her chintz petticoat had always been
a hindrance to me, and also her snuff-
box, and I so often had to begin all over
again.

At first she seemed rather hurt at the
request; but then I began to cry, and
pleaded that baby looked so dear; and she
consented, and called us "Poor innocents!"
and began to cry too.

Piers was asleep, one little arm under his

round cheek, flushed as it was with sleep, and the other little fat hand clenched like a wrestler's, and thrust out over the edge of his cot. My prayers must have been a mysterious ritual to me, scarcely "in a tongue understanded of the people." No one had ever explained them to me. I do not remember ever expecting anything to come of them, except some vague harm to some one if they were left out. What the words were at that time I cannot even tell. There were no Sunday-schools in our town ; nurse was very ignorant, and I am sure she could not read. Not improbably they were the Lord's Prayer and the invocation to the Four Evangelists, long afterwards not disused in the district. And my theology was, doubtless, neither definite nor broad. It certainly, however, included a belief in Something that could hurt Piers and me, especially if we were naughty, and in the dark.

But mysterious indeed are all little children's prayers!

Who knows the "tongues of angels?" Who knows the mystic, unutterable communion there may be between the Father of spirits and those little ones whose angels always see his face!

"Exiled children of Eve," little royal strangers, whose wondering eyes have not yet narrowed their range to our mortal vision,—whose free, fearless, questioning thought is not yet fettered to our mortal speech,—who knows the delicate, aerial touches that come and go along those strings the world's rude hands have not yet swept? Who knows the moment when the Father who fell on the prodigal's neck and kissed him, clasps to his heart those little ones who have not yet wilfully left the Father's house? what kisses, what consecrating touches are theirs?

Who knows, since God is love,—not primarily the Infinite Mind that speaks to us by works or thoughts, but the Father's heart that speaks to us by loving,—what divine touches, real as a mother's kisses, tender as the soft pressure of her arms, rest on the little ones?

Not only on a few score of exceptional little Galilean children were the sacred Hands laid, in those three years' which made visible the eternity of unseen Divine love.

Nor is it only a few Jewish fishermen who have misunderstood the love of the Master for little children,—the babes,—the creatures we call speechless and unconscious.

Is it not rather *we* who have become blind, and speechless, and unconscious? blinded by the countless small glitterings, and the countless vain pryings of this world; robbed of heavenly utterance by its empty chatterings and bitter contentions;

made unconscious by its drowsy charms, of
the realities of life and death, and love, of
the capacities for sorrow and joy, deeper
even than sorrow around and within us still,
whether we know it or not,—as they are
around the little children we think unaware
of them?

Who knows how little the wisest of us
know, or how much the simplest?

I know not, indeed, what passed in my
heart that night, or what words passed my
lips. But I remember my cheek resting on
my little brother's cheek, and the dear little
hand unclenching itself and resting on me,
and the sleepy eyes opening for a moment
on mine, and the parted lips sleepily lisping
my name.

And I remember lying down in my own
little bed afterwards, so still and happy, and
warm at heart, feeling not so much that I
was brooded over, or needed it, as that some
kind of wings had unfolded in me, and were

brooding over Piers, and keeping him safe and warm.

That was, as far as I can remember, the way God began to teach me; by filling my heart with that great love which was just a little feeble image of His.

CHAPTER III.

IN these days to be Insular is a reproach which most people repel with indignation· Or if anyone admits it with a contemptuous pity as but too applicable, in many respects, to our country, it is always with the tacit understanding that he himself is contemplating that narrow and common-place little community from some wide continent of experience and thought whence the island and its interests assume their duly diminutive proportions.

In my early days, people gloried in being Insular. The " right little, tight little island " was delighted in with something of the same kind of attachment an old sailor used to feel for his ship—knowing well her weak points, but knowing also what storms she had weathered, what broadsides she had gallantly stood, and how fearless she was as to the tempests and battles to come; a patriotism not at all tending to anything international or cosmopolitan, but combative, exclusive, Insular to the core.

The Americans were still our " colonies " across the seas; we were fresh from a hot fight with them, in which our national temper had not been sweetened by our having been in the wrong and having been beaten. On most of us the idea had scarcely dawned that they were a Nation at all. They were " our plantations," a branch of the old trunk, vigorous certainly, but very knotty, and gnarled; the vigour of course belonging to the stock they came of, and (perhaps it must be admitted) the knots and gnarls also. The echoes of a hundred years before, moreover, had scarcely died away, and in some Englishmen resentment against "rebels" who had

disowned the king was blended with a dim
disapproval of Dissenters who had tried to
upset the Church, and were believed for the
most part to be Puritans (whatever that
meant), and therefore, naturally, to speak
through their noses.

Again, the French were "a nation of dancing masters," who, with all their misplaced
agility, could not climb the shrouds of a ship.
Had not their own Voltaire lately called them
a compound of monkey and tiger?

The "German States"—(Germany did not
exist, even in popular ballads)—were too
remote, and too unknown and varying a
quantity to have any definite portrait.

Spain loomed mistily on us, gigantic and
yet shadowy, with the old glooms and glories
of her past playing fitfully around her, her
palaces and prisons still echoing, as we believed, with groans under an Inquisition
not yet dead; her fleets still recalling the
Armada; yet through all, a ghastliness and

ghostliness, as if the whole structure were held together by old spells grown feeble, and at a bold touch or word might crumble helplessly away.

Insular! we thanked God in our hymns for it; islanded safe, in our green security, with our glorious constitution in Church and State, our King, our Church, our "wooden walls;" a second "chosen people," better preserved than the first from the various idolatrous nations around. If Israel of old had been guarded by the Straits of Dover and the German Ocean, who could say that things might not have ended differently? But no doubt it was to be. Israel was a stiff-necked people, and we, on the contrary, were always improving ourselves and our constitution.

Of course even then there were a few croakers, who might have repeated Oliver Cromwell's old exhortation, " You glory in that ditch which guards your shores; I tell you your ditch will be no defence to you un-

less you reform yourselves ; " and a few profane wits infected with the levity of France,
who did not regard even the Thirty-nine
Articles, or our most religious and gracious
king as unassailable ; and a few democrats
who did not consider even our glorious constitution final.   But for the most part, even
if when comparing class with class amongst
us, we now and then recognised reluctantly
that there was some unequal pressure, that
there might be some corners which were not
quite paradise ; when, on the other hand,
we compared ourselves with the rest of the
world, our self appreciation was restored, and
we became once more sensible of our privi-
leges.

Moreover, not only were we one island,
we were in another sense an archipelago of
islands.

Not only was England thus islanded
from the world. Every country town was
islanded from the rest—was a living com-

munity in itself, with its own local history and government, local glories and wrongs, its local circles of families, established there for generations; not certainly without their mutual jealousies and rivalries, but belonging to each other, by a real and recognised relationship.

And still farther within this inner island was an innermost, like the ball within ball of an Indian ivory puzzle.

In those days every Englishman's " house was his castle," in a more peculiar sense, or at least in a greater variety of senses, than now. A house belonged to a family, was part of its complex existence, more in the same sense than a man's body is part of his complex self. It grew with the family growth, flourished with the family prosperity, decayed with the family decay; and as we die out of our bodies and leave them, so, with a mortality in one sense more pathetic because apparently not inevitable, a family might, by misfortune, folly, failure of succession, die out of the old family house. A house, therefore, had quite a different significance; it had family histories stamped into it, growing out of it; it had features, characteristics, a life of its own.

There are stately mansions of our great families, to which something of this character attaches still. The greatness and glory of the great family is built into them, and they stand.

But then, this family character attached to countless unpretending English houses, and this not only in country places, to fine old manorial halls, or homely farmsteads, but in the streets of every town. We all of us can recognise these old houses still. They look out on us with pathetic or quaint and humorous human faces; the humanity that has grown with them and around them, and from them for generations, cannot die out of them. And when we see them left stranded and forlorn in some featureless row of windows and doors, such as human creatures now swarm and are fed in, until the next hive is ready, we welcome them or compassionate them, not as buildings but as friends.

In such houses were the families of my childhood islanded in the island of our little country town, in the island of our England.

I smile sometimes a little when I see people endeavouring now æsthetically to restore this lost sacredness of houses by means of Elizabethan windows and fireplaces, and mediæval texts, and family arms on doors and walls, I think the rush of nineteenth century life will be too strong for them. Will their children live where they lived, or love what they loved, or think as they thought?

If it is hard to make a lost religion or a lost architecture live again, I think it is harder still to revive a dead habit of social life. But our grandchildren will see.

It is this inmost island of home that I must

first picture, before the scene widens to the town and the country in which it was enclosed. All true geography, all geography which would lead to the knowledge, not of names, but of things, must begin, not with the ecliptic and the equator, but with the pond in our own farmyard.

The living germ of our town was a Benedictine abbey, one of the finest and earliest in the kingdom. This abbey had been built by the side of a clear, rocky river, where the hills through which it cut its way from the moorland opened out so as to leave a little level of rich meadow land.

Around the church and the conventual buildings, the two solid stone bridges, and the weir with its deep pool and salmon trap, whence the town Abbot's Weir had its name, the houses of the town clustered, gradually stretching back over the strip of level to the hills.

Our house had thus been driven to the

foot of the steep slope, and had been constrained to make the best of it by all kinds of
eccentric devices, climbing here and delving
there, until it possessed scarcely two rooms
on the same level; to children perhaps the
most delightful plan on which a house could
be constructed. Its very existence was a
continual victory over adverse circumstances,
and tended to communicate to its inhabitants,
according to the material on which the stamp
was impressed, a character either militant
and adventurous, or easy and imperturbable,
conquering circumstance by resolutely sur-
mounting it, or by accepting its ups and downs
as inevitable, and making them part of its
own constitution.

The entrance was by a Tudor arch into a
broad passage. On the right was a large
wainscoted room with a stone floor and one
long, low mullioned window with a long,
deep window-seat. In this room, as a rule,
the family breakfasted, dined, and had all

its family meals—all, that were not connected with ceremonial, and extended to
strangers. This also was the nearest approach Piers and I had to a day nursery or
playroom, our great resource on any wet
days which drove us from our natural ter-
ritory in the garden; a room into which,
even after the *régime* of my stepmother,
Pluto was admitted, and my father's fa-
vourite pointer and setter, and that long
succession of my kittens which came to such
a variety of tragical ends. Mrs. Danescombe's cat, which never came to misfortune
of any kind, sleek, impenetrable, demure,
resided in the Oak Parlour, approached by
a small flight of steps on the opposite side of
the passage. Into this we only went by
invitation; but that cat had the .*entrée*. A
most evil and hypocritical creature we considered her; an embodiment of all the dark
side of cat-nature—malignantly breaking
all the china and gluttonously imbibing all

the dainties (on account of which my luck-less kittens suffered), and then sitting up-right on the parlour window-seat winking superciliously at all the world.

There were few middle tints in the por-traits of our childhood, and among the most Rembrandt-like that comes back to me is the image of my stepmother's cat. All that Puritan meant to the most prejudiced of Cavaliers, or Tartuffe to the most anti-ecclesiastical of Frenchmen, that sleek, stealthy, whiskered black-and-white cat meant to me. It scarcely ever purred. We believed it could not purr; its conscience was too laden with crime. Nor do I re-member its ever playing, except once or twice in a murderous way with a fly on the window-pane when it thought no one was looking. Its name was Mignonette, and to this day I can scarcely do justice to the sweetness of the little flower whose appella-tion it polluted.

The Oak Parlour had a very different social rank from the Stone Parlour. It was my stepmother's especial domain. It was seldom entered by any one until the afternoon, being the scene of leisurely employment and sober amusement, and of all social entertainments not of the stateliest kind. There Mrs. Danescombe embroidered muslin and made lace, or took snuff and played cards with chosen associates, always for small stakes; and there were solemnly handed around trays with small glasses of liqueurs or cordials, or in aftertimes with dainty small cups of tea. No uproarious merriment was ever heard within those precincts; nothing stronger than tea or cordials was ever sipped therein. Seldom did masculine foot invade them. If my father wished to entertain his friends with solid British viands and vigorous British beverages, recourse was had to the Stone Parlour, where also we gathered in the winter evenings on oaken settles or foot-stools around the great old chimney with its dogs and log-fires. Echoes of Christmas merriment and of children's laughter hung around those old walls; but the wainscoting of the Oak Parlour could never have reported anything more sonorous than the murmured gossip of the card-table, unless some of the players by any series of other people's mistakes or their own mischances lost their games and their tempers, and broke out of the decorum of the place into the hard realities of unfairly lost shillings and sixpences.

There were two sacred things to me, however, in the room.

In the recesses on each side of the high oaken chimneypiece with its carved looking-glass, hung portraits of my father and of my own mother in the dresses they wore just after they were married: he with a bag-wig, hand ruffles, and a sword, and

elaborate shoe-buckles, which certainly did
not recall his every-day appearance; she
with powdered hair brushed over a high
cushion, a little hat stuck coquettishly on
the top of it, a blue satin bodice and train,
and brocaded petticoat, with a large bou-
quet in the hand laid on her lap, and a
shepherd's crook in the other. At her feet
was a lamb wreathed with flowers, looking
wistfully up in her face. The native Van-
dyke or Sir Joshua had evidently a confused
Ideal compounded of the pastoral and the
courtly, and was very familiar with neither.
There must have been something very in-
vincible in the character of my mother's
face to penetrate as it did at once through
the false idealism and the imperfect exe-
cution of the painter. For it was evidently
a likeness. Underneath a fair, finely-arched
brow were distinct though delicate eyebrows, visible far back at the side of the
forehead, and overshadowing very large,

soft dark-grey eyes. There was much depth in the eyes, but no dreaminess. They evidently *saw*—saw the lamb looking up into them, and much besides. The mouth was firm and grave; the pose of the whole figure was at once easy and commanding; the small hand, wooden as the painting was, held the crook with a real grasp. You felt instinctively that the visible lamb and the imaginary flock were well cared for under such guardianship. Oh! with what longing I used to look at that lamb lying so safe at her feet!

She sate before me a type not so much of fond, passionate motherliness, as of tender, wise, protective motherhood; not so much of the mother's bliss, as of the mother's care; not like one of Murillo's girl Madonnas dreaming over a new delight, but like one of the earlier Italian school, grave with the very weight of the mother's joy, and with the destinies of the life with which her own was bound up.

For had I not the memory of her touch
and her kiss to interpret the portrait? Had
not those hands pressed me to her heart,
and did I not know how those grave lips
could part and smile?

Underneath this portrait stood a little
table with a well in it, containing, I knew,
my mother's work, and especially one dainty
little frill of a baby's cap, unfinished, with
her needle in it. Upon it was placed her
ebony spinning-wheel. Nurse used to dust
it reverently every morning; and often I
stole in with her, and then, when nurse was
not looking, I used to reach up to the
picture and softly kiss its hands.

Every afternoon, when there was no company, I spent an hour in that room with
Mrs. Danescombe and the hypocritical cat,
learning to sew. But at those times I did not
dare to look much at my beloved picture;
because, being frequently in trouble with
my work, I was afraid if I caught sight of

that lamb and of that dear face, a terrible
rush of the feeling of motherlessness would
come over me, and I should cry. For, once,
when I had been very unsuccessful with my
sewing, and had had to unpick it several
times, this had happened, and Mrs. Danescombe had asked what I was crying for;
and I, stretching out my arms to the picture, and sobbing out something about
"mother," my stepmother had replied in
an even, undisturbed voice—one of her
maxims being that "a gentlewoman never
degrades reproof into scolding by raising
her voice "—

"Bridget, this is something I cannot per-
mit. When little girls lose their tempers
over their tasks, I cannot suffer them to
deceive themselves by calling their naughty
passions sensibility. You have many faults,
but I did hope you were a truthful child.
Never let me hear you speak in that way
again."

And that was a reproach I never did incur again. How it burnt into my heart! Not only by the injustice, but the justice in it. For I was a very truthful child; and it was not only the dull pain of being misunderstood that hurt me; it was the terrible fear that my stepmother, after all, had understood me better than I understood myself. Was she not older, wiser, my father's chosen ruler for us—set over us by all the mysterious powers whence authority springs—authority against which I had not a thought of rebelling? And had I not been in something very like a naughty temper, writing down very hard things against my stepmother, and the bitter fate of little girls in general who had to learn sewing, indeed, even against the Nature of Things which involved clothes that had to be sewn? And was it possible that I had desecrated that love to my own mother, and the memory of her love, by making it an excuse even to myself for being cross and angry?

I certainly had sometimes underneath these perplexities and self-accusations a dim sense, now and then flashing into a passionate persuasion, that it was *not* all my fault. But then I reproached myself again for this.

If the things in Mrs. Danescombe's character which jarred against mine had been angles, the conflict would have been less harassing. But in her there were no angles; there was nothing to lay hold of; it was simply coldness, smoothness of surface, hard polish, and impenetrability; and what "case" could be made out of these? She never scolded, or threatened, or punished. She simply reproved. Her severest discipline was a distant politeness and a peculiar way of calling me "Bridget." What was cruel in that? Yet it froze into my bones. And there were times when her

mere presence was to me a prison worse
than the darkest of the dark holes nurse
threatened us with. It was not until long
afterwards that I learned why.

Her government was based on suspicion.
She was not theological in any sense; she
had no extreme theories of the depravity
of human nature. But she had a deep-
seated conviction that every man and
woman, and more especially every servant
and little child, was more likely to do
wrong than right, and more likely to
do wrong from the worst motives than the
best.

Combined with this, or perhaps flowing
from it, was a remarkable keenness of perception as to any defect or mistake, in anything or person, from a speck of dust or
rust on the furniture, to the smallest sole-
cism in dress or manners, or the least excess
or defect in demeanour.

Therefore she never praised; partly because she thought commendation nourished vanity, and partly because in the best work she always detected some petty blemish, not imaginary, but real; yet, however small, sufficient to distract her attention from all that was good in it.

It would be a difficult atmosphere to *grow* in, but that we had a large space of life free from her inspection, and an element of positive freedom, warmth, and breadth in my father, which I suppose would scarcely have done alone.

Only I have often thought that my mother's character would have been the supplementary opposite, as my stepmother's was the neutralising contrary of my father. My mother's character would have drawn out and filled up all that was highest and best in his. Mrs. Danescombe merely repressed and neutralised. With her he was, perhaps, restrained from doing or saying some things better not done or said; with my mother he would have become all he might have been. Both made some kind of harmony, but with my mother all the life would have been larger, richer, fuller.

CHAPTER IV.

AT the end of the passage was a wide
stair-case with black oak banisters,
which led to the Best Parlour, an apartment
provided with furniture altogether

> " too bright and good
> For common nature's daily food;"

where from week to week the amber damask
curtains and tapestried chairs were pinned
into thick coverings, and the carpet was
rolled up on one side, and the gilded sconces
on the frame of the small round looking-
glass was veiled, and the Venetian-blinds
were closely shut.

This was the inmost sanctuary of Mrs.
Damescombe's domain. In my mother's time
it had not been furnished, and I had faint

memories of its having been abandoned to us as a play-room, of wild games played there with my father in winter twilight, and of delicious terrors, half real and half feigned, as he sprang on us from dim corners with awful growls and roars, in the characters of lion or bear. Moreover outside there was a balcony which was a delightfully romantic place, whence the world assumed quite a new aspect, a border land which was neither in-doors nor out-of-doors, where all the life of the street moved before us in a continual pro-cession, better than any picture-book.

But now all this was changed, and we only entered the room at all on the very highest days in our very best, and therefore most harassing, clothes; and would as soon have thought of venturing into the pulpit of the church as into the balcony.

Behind this were the principal bedrooms, looking on an inner court, and then a flight of rather ladder-like stairs leading to the

first platform of the garden, on which opened
the Summer Parlour.   This was my father's
especial retreat, the corner of the house which
he succeeded in defending against all the as-
saults of order, and keeping freely open to us.

In this room we had the rights of citizen-
ship to the fullest extent; everything was
open to us; and, in consequence, everything
was sacred to us.   We were trusted and believed in; and to have hurt anything my
father cared about, would have been to Piers
or me, naturally, the direst of misfortunes.

My father's principles of government and
views of life were the very contrary to Mrs.
Danescombe's.   His expectation was that
every one belonging to him would do right.
and everything would go right; and if, contrary to expectation, any one did wrong, or
anything went wrong, he was wont to attri-
bute it to the best possible motives, and re-
sume his sanguine anticipations unbroken.
Not perhaps, an altogether adequate principle

for government on any large scale. Although I remember being smitten with a far keener repentance by being misunderstood by him on the too favourable side than all my step-mother's keen detection and exposure of the dark side ever brought to me.

The real defect in his rule was not, I think, hoping or trusting too much, but suffering his sanguine temperament to dim his sight. To see everything that is wrong, and yet hope everything good, is higher, I suppose, because truer.

And it was there, I fancy, my mother would have helped him. The optimism which revolted to an extreme against Mrs. Danescombe's suspicions would have been braced and corrected by my mother's loving truthfulness.

That room was a world of interest to us. There were marvellous models of machines in it (those were the days of Watt and Ark-wright), balls of twine, fishing tackle, carpenters' tools, a turning lathe, pieces of various woods—Spanish mahogany and cedar, curious knots and blocks of oak, box, walnut, and various native woods; for my father delighted in experimenting, and had a theory that half the use that might be was not made of our own English produce. The marred work, and the pieces with unconquerable flaws, were our Jetsam and Flotsam; but the greatest pleasure of all was to be allowed to stand by and watch while he was at work.

To watch the real work of grown people was an endless interest to us children. It was their amusements, and still more their attempts to amuse us, which seemed to us so dull. And by mistaken benevolence of that kind we in our childhood were not much oppressed.

My father having much " of the child's heart in his breast," took us quite naturally into his confidence, and enjoyed our sympathy in his projects, as much as we did his

in ours. Mrs. Danescombe, probably never
having known childhood herself, capable of
having existed from infancy like the children
in old-fashioned family pictures, erect from
morning till night in a cushion and hoop,
never thought of us as helpless creatures that
had to be made happy, but as fallen and re-
fractory creatures that had to be kept down,
and brought up, and if possible kept tidy.
Thus no one took any trouble to amuse us.
And accordingly we were endlessly amused.

Never, moreover, were children happier in
the scenery of their childhood, than we in that
dear old up and down house and garden.

The garden consisted of a succession of
platforms and terraces, connected by flights
of steps or by steep slopes. The first of these
was opposite the Summer Parlour. Round
it was a border of flowers—roses, pansies,
marigolds, love-lies-bleeding, hen and chicken
daisies, sunflowers, hollyhocks, all Lord
Bacon's catalogue. In one corner, hollowed

out of the rocky hill-side, was a Dropping Well, where the slow falling of the drops, one by one, we saw not whence, into the dark, cool water below, mysteriously echoing from the sides, made sweet music for us. The entrance was draped by tufts and fringes of ferns of the richest green and the most delicate forms; beneath it, under the rock, was a bed of the sweetest lilies of the valley. It was only entered in the early morning by a few stray sunbeams, and of these scarcely one reached the opposite rock, and none ever penetrated into the clefts and corners.

My father told us it was natural, and carved out by the little drops themselves dropping through hundreds, perhaps thousands of years. They had begun their chimes, he said, long before any had sounded from the old church-tower.

Thus to us that little melodious well was like the threshold of a thousand delightful mysteries. Where did those melodious drops

start from ? From what dark hidden pools
under the hills ? from what bright, floating
clouds in the sky ? Whose pitchers had they
filled,—what little children had they sung to
before ? What were they saying to us, or
wanting to say ? Wistful Undines and
Nixen longing to speak to us; wise busy
gnomes at work for ages, knowing thousands
of secrets they would not tell but we would
give anything to hear; all the wild mythology of mountain and water sprites; all that
"nurse" Nature would say to us and cannot;
all that we would learn from her and cannot;
dim reflections of our human life on material
things; dim shinings through and prismatic
refractions of the Divine life beyond and
within; all this and unutterably more murmured to us through that Dropping Well.
Children of the mystic and humorous North,
did we need legends Scandinavian or Teutonic to tell us what a strange compound the
world was ?

Was there not, moreover, from time to time, in that very well, an apparition of a gigantic wide-mouthed frog, who in the midst of all that melancholy and mystic music, and those delicate ferns, and those sweet lilies of the valley, would croak and hop, and be as self-satisfied, and as entirely an embodied joke as any of quaintest dwarfs Grim ever disinterred or Cruikshank ever drew; the whole mysterious animal world lay open to us between our sympathetic dog Pluto and that supercilious, impenetrable frog.

When years afterwards we saw these German stories, we felt we had known them all our lives.

For I confess I am tempted to count it among the blessings of our childhood that we had no children's books at all.

No doubt there were children's books in our days; but the allowance was scanty, and what there were did not reach us. If we had been provided with any, they would, no doubt, have been heavily weighted with morals, and would have been duller to us than our lessons. But, happily, we were not. Our lesson books were good, honest lesson books— my first was a horn-book. Our alphabets had no pictures; there was no sugar on the margin of our draughts of learning. We took them, certainly not without tears. But if to us " books" meant the antithesis of " play," and we cried over them and their consequences very heartily and very frequently, at least we did not fall into the far more desperate fate of yawning over our play, and listlessly requesting to be instructed how to amuse ourselves.

In our days the age of wise children's literature had not commenced. For us Rosamond and Frank, Harry and Lucy did not exist. They may, indeed, have dawned on some of the higher social summits, but certainly did not penetrate to Abbot's Weir. Still less, of course, was there anything for us of the nature of the reactionary literature of nonsense, clever or inane, which succeeded that era of præternatural good sense.

What nursery nonsense we had was quite genuine, with no perplexing parodies of sense, or half glimmerings of sense treacherously lurking beneath the surface. For us Little Jack Horner sate in his corner, and took out his plum, and congratulated himself (not as one might have expected, on his good fortune, but on his virtue), in the most literal way, without any allegorical construction. No suspicions of satire, or of the signs of the zodiac, marred our enjoyment of the confusion which ensued when "the cat had the fiddle, the cow jumped over the moon, the little dog laughed to see the sport, and the dish ran away with the spoon."

For us Mother Hubbard's agreeable disappointment at the futility of her dog's coffin was always fresh; the funeral rites of Jenny Wren could be repeated to any extent; the Babes in the Wood and Little Red Riding Hood were alternately dreaded and desired as we felt equal or not to the luxuries of tragedy. But between those ancient histories and the literature of our elders there was no intervening world of little boys and girls, exemplarily good, præternaturally naughty, sentimental, religious, or scientific.

The world of grown people's work—of animals and flowers, the garden, and the Timber-yard, and the Iron Foundry were our books. And for us there was no idle reading.

But perhaps we were exceptionally happy in these respects. My father himself was our Miss Edgeworth, almost always ready to explain to us his own work, or to enter with such serious interest as we felt its due into ours.

And, of course, it is not every child who can be free of a Timber-yard and a Foundry as we were.

For I have not yet told half the delights of our garden.

By the side of the Dropping Well was a door, better to us than any underground step of Aladdin, leading through a short tunnel, ending in a flight of stairs cut in the rock, to the second garden, which was a steep slope crowned at the top with a terrace and an arbour.

This was of peculiar interest to us, because it was one of the pages of our own original illustrated copy of the Pilgrim's Progress, being obviously the Hill Difficulty, the arbour where Christian lost his roll, and also in another aspect the Palace Beautiful, and the Delectable Mountains whence the pilgrims could survey the land.

Could not we survey the whole land from that summit?

Below us lay the slate roofs of the town, tier below tier, the two bridges and the

river; and opposite was the fine old grey
tower of the church, with its pinnacles
standing out against the wooded hillsides,
whilst above stretched the sweeping curves
and sharp angles of the granite Tors, the
moorland hills, whence the river flowed,
purple and golden, with crisp lights and
shadows, or, blue and soft and far away,
"the everlasting hills."

This, therefore, was one of our usual
haunts on Sunday afternoons.

In the side wall of this garden was
another door, and beyond it an orchard,
and beyond that a great free range of fields
called the Leas, and at the top of this a
channel of water called the Leat, which
was detached higher up from the river, and
fell at one end of the Leas in a cascade
which turned the large water-wheel of the
Iron Foundry. At the other end of this
field was the Timber-yard, and the Foundry and the Timber-yard were among the

chief scenes of my father's work and our play.

In those days it was the general custom for men of business to live near their work. Now, scarcely even the smaller shopkeepers live over their shops; and not only great cities but country towns are fringed with their suburbs of villas. Then, even large merchants lived near their warehouses, and if, as we did, they possessed a farm, it was a genuine farm, in the real country, where men and women did their real work; and if things were fair to see, it was because it was their nature, not because they were put there to be seen. I suppose there is gain in the change. People breathe better air, at least physically; of the moral atmosphere I am not so sure. It may be good to escape from the cares of business to vineries and conservatories and geranium beds; it is certainly better than to be buried, body and soul, in business; but to ennoble business is even better than to escape from it. All work must be degraded and must degrade, the chief object of which is to earn the means to do no work. The highest art may certainly in that way be degraded into a trade; and I think there are few manufactures or trades which may not, on the other hand, be raised into art.

At least it was so with my father. That Timber-yard and that Foundry were to him, and through him to us, outlets into the world of knowledge and of work.

Into the interior of the Foundry we were not permitted to enter except under his protection.

My chief associations with that were a sense of the wonder-working powers of Water and of Fire.

It was, indeed, a perpetual fairy tale to see those creatures which we knew as fantastic dwarfs, or melodious melancholy nymphs, or dancing sprites, when they worked at their own wild will in the Dropping Well, or around the great logs on the hearth of the Stone Parlour, transformed into steadfast and irresistible giants by the pressure of the steady will of man.

For thousands of years the slow dropping water had been at work, and had carved out to the sound of its own singing that strange hollow in the rocky hills, with its grotesque angles and dim clefts ; and now at last the great water-wheel was set to direct it, and patiently and willingly the mighty creature, rising to its full strength, turned the great machine round and round, making by its own unconquerable beauty the loveliest sparkling cascades and showers at every turn. And out of this combined power, of water and man, came harrows, and spades, and scythes ; and pots, and pans, and kettles, and all kinds of fairy household gifts to make our work easier and our homes pleasanter. Were not the swift, flashing waters careering with their rush of rapid music over the wheel as pleasant to see and hear as when dropping into the well? And were not scythes and even kettles as poetical things to make as caves?—the fireside and the reaping field being surely as sacred as the rocky hillside and the heathery moors?

I have always, however, been rather glad, as far as the lessons and associations of childhood went, that our machinery was worked by the separate powers of Fire and Water, and not by these powers combined, in the more prosaic form of Steam.

There was a large foundry not fifty miles from us, worked by steam, before we were born. And at the great engine factory of Boulton and Watt, many years before, my father used to tell how Mr. Boulton showed Dr. Johnson round, and said to him, "Sir, we sell here the thing all men are in search of—power."

We lived in the days of the birth and infancy of many things which have since grown to gigantic powers and overspread the world.

Our childhood was passed in one of the great dawns of history. The world was awake and stirring around us in every direction — machinery, politics, religion ; and my father was a man awake to every throb of the busy life around him.

The great Steam Power was already in the world, and through the busy brains of Watt, Cartwright, and Arkwright was feeling after its work in railroads, steamboats, and power-looms. But happily for us, our moorland river did the work for us, and instead of pistons and cranks and close oily rooms, we had our gigantic water-wheel and the cascade which rushed over it from the hill.

Then, the pictures and parables enacted for us on the great casting-days, when we

were taken to see the molten metal flow
out of the furnace into the moulds of sand,
the Rembrandt-like groups of men with
blackened, illumined faces shovelling out
the liquid fire as if they had been agents
in some fiery horrors of Dante's Inferno;
the power of heat in that red cave of fire
raging at its roof into fierce white flames,
which always made me think of Nebuchad-
nezzar's fiery furnace, and clasp tight my
father's hand and Piers,' lest they should be
burned up like the wicked executioners !

I used to wonder how the three children
and that " Fourth " looked in the midst
of the flames; not black, I was sure, like
old Reuben Pengelly, the furnace-man, but
beautiful and calm, and fresh and white,
like a very bright soft moon in the midst of
the angry glare.

Yet old Reuben himself was very dear
to us children. He had lost a little boy
about the age of Piers, and he had always

a very tender feeling to Piers, partly because the child, looking, no doubt, from
his blackened face, and muscular bare neck,
to his kind eyes, had always had such
trust in him, and would have gone in his
arms to the mouth of the furnace. Reuben's
delight on Sunday, when he had his clean
washed face, and his best coat on, was to
carry Piers in his arms about the silent
foundry-yard, amongst the stationary wheels
and hammers, and to sing us Methodist
hymns. For he was a man of a strong,
fervent piety, such as fitted his rough work
and his muscular frame; and it was from
him I first remember hearing the story of
the three children in the furnace. To
Reuben the Bible was the written part of
a continuous living history, unwritten; and
he told us how that Fourth, "who made
the flames as soft as morning dew to them,
was with him, old Reuben Pengelly, as
really as with them, and with us little

ones, too." And I used often to gaze into
the depths of that burning haze, in a vague
hope of finding something marvellous there.

All the men knew us, not as angelic
benefactors descending on them now and
then on festival occasions, but as little
creatures they had some kind of tender right
in; "master's," and also therefore "theirs."
And we knew the inside of many of their
homes, not merely by religious or benevolent visits, but naturally, as our *neighbours*, as people who had known and loved
and served us and ours before we had
known them.

There is incalculably much in that tie
of neighbourhood between rich and poor,
employer and employed. The mere daily
natural crossing of our paths is something,
the familiarity with each other's faces and
dwellings, and the countless kindnesses
that may spring out of it, are infinitely
more. Our Lord knew us well when He

said, not, " Ye shall love mankind as yourselves," but, " Thou shalt love thy neighbour as thyself." We often read it the
other way. But the meaning is quite
different.

And it often seems to me that half the
social problems which beset us arise from
the rich and poor having ceased in so many
instances to be neighbours. What is half
at least of our charitable machinery but
an ineffectual and clumsy effort to replace
the countless little interchanges of mutual
good-will and service, the countless health-
ful, mutually sustaining intertwinings of
life and love, which are involved in the
simple fact of living within sight of each
other ?

The Timber-yard, however, was Piers'
and my most constant resource and delight; our gymnasium, our race-course, the
dockyard of our navies.

Thence also the histories my father told

us made a broad channel on which our imaginations sailed away to the various northern and southern lands, where the great bare timbers over which we sprang had grown.

When we were tired we used to sit on these trunks, and Piers would listen to any extent whilst I reproduced to him narratives of bears and wolves which had crept stealthily like cats over the snows after their prey, or howled and growled among the stems of these Norway pines.

We must have been rather sensational and gloomy in our tastes, for these bear and wolf stories were always more popular with us than those of the garlanded trees, and gay parrots, or even of the monkeys of the south. Through the Timber-yard, the atlas became a living world to us; and I have no doubt the sense of all those far-off things and creatures mingled like music with our play, as we jumped from trunk to trunk, as free and happy as the squirrels and birds which had hopped from branch to branch in former days.

Here also were the chips out of which we constructed the fleets which sailed in the Leat at the top of the Leas, the fleets for which we made harbours and piers, and carried on our great contest with the elements that were always ruthlessly endeavouring to draw them over the cascade, to be crushed by the inexorable water-wheel.

CHAPTER V.

THE Sundays of our childhood, how much depends on them! To me the associations they bring are chiefly of sunshine and rest; undisturbed, unless by an uneasy sense of responsibility in relation to Sunday clothes.

I cannot recall much definite religious teaching. We used, certainly, to say the Church Catechism to Mrs. Danescombe: and I must confess it seemed to me a very obscure collocation of words, in which it was nearly impossible not to put the wrong sentence first. I do not remember any part of it being explained to us, except the duty to our Neighbour, which was enforced on us with strong personal application, and

left me so oppressed with the impossibility
of either saying or doing it, and so perplexed about the quantity of wrong things
one might have done without knowing, that
I should have been quite ready, with a
certain little French girl at her first confession, to have pronounced myself guilty
of all the sins prohibited in the Decalogue,
including Simony.

My father never gave us direct lessons
of any kind, religious or secular. He was
undoubtedly not didactic, and I suppose
he was not dogmatic; probably not finding
any great necessity of formulas for his own
use, and certainly not disposed to impose
them on others. Neither was he given to
cavil or to question. His mind was as
little of the stuff heretics as of that in-
quisitors are made of; a subtle material,
perhaps sometimes more similar than either
think. In Scotland I think it probable
he would have accepted the Westminster

Confession, in Saxony the Confession of
Augsburg, in France the great Creeds of
the Gallican Church, his faith in all cases
remaining substantially the same, and in
all cases omitting the anathemas.

He was not theological at all in the sense
of being keenly alive to the defects in other
people's theology. He was theological to
the core in the sense that St. John was the
Theologian; in that his faith began with
God rather than with man; less with man,
erring, falling, sinning, than with God,
loving, giving, forgiving.

Analysis and criticism were not his element. So far from his theology being
negative, if anything was wanting in it,
it was negations. If in after life we
wandered into doubts and perplexities,
to come back to him was to come back
neither to elaborate solutions nor to anxious
denunciations, but to the child's heart and
the Apostles' Creed. His influence on us

was through what he was, and what he loved.

Cowper, then a new poet, was his delight; not for his satire on social frailties, or his bitter lamentations over human depravity; but for his sympathy for human wrong, his gentle pathos, his sunny humour, his large and loving hope in man and God.

Not that my father was destitute of the force of indignation; but, like Cowper's, his indignation was reserved for injustice rather than for error; for the Bastille, for the slave-trade, for the desecration of the sacrament into a political test, for the corruption and meanness of " corporations," for "charging God with such outrageous wrong " as leaving the sages of old

> " in endless woe
> For ignorance of what they could not know."

It is strange to see how many abuses then hotly contended for, are now abandoned by the extremest reactionists; and on the other hand, how much of the larger hopes which still have to be contended for, had even then dawned on generous Christian hearts.

To my father we owe the blessing of liberation, space, and joyousness connected with Sunday; and to him also the inestimable benefit that to us Christianity was associated, not with limitation, prohibition, and retrogression, but with freedom, expansion, and progress, with all that is generous and glad and hopeful, and belonging to the light.

At eight o'clock the "warning" church bell announced that it was Sunday; and father used to knock at our nursery door, and carry us off to the weekly festival of breakfast in the Stone Parlour, Piers usually perched on his shoulders, and I holding his hand.

Then followed that long trial of patience, —the apparelling for church; and then the

walk by father's side down the quiet yet
festive street, between the closed shop windows, among the friendly greetings of the
neighbours, across the churchyard, past that
one corner of it which was the most sacred
place on earth to him and to us, up the long
aisle to our high square pew, between the
Squire's and the Vicar's.

When we sate down my view was neces-
sarily quite domestic, limited by the wooden
walls. But when the singing began, it was
my privilege to stand on the seat and
survey the congregation; and most marvellous and interesting to me were the
Sunday transformations of everybody by
means of clothes.

There was far more difference between
best and every-day clothes in those days
than now, and far more variety in costume,
not only between different classes—between
what might be generally termed rich and
poor—but between the different orders and

species of well-to-do people. Between the rich and poor the contrast was not only in form but in material. Silk was utterly unknown below a certain level; calico prints with imitations of French or Damascene patterns had not been made common by Manchester looms. Stout wolseys, woven in cottage looms, clean white kerchiefs, and sober blues and hodden greys characterized the free-seats.

Yet none of the transformations of Sunday seemed to me so complete and remarkable as that which set Reuben Pengelly in the choir gallery embracing a huge musical instrument—not the " wee sinfu' fiddle," but a gigantic bass-viol—in a bright blue coat and scarlet waistcoat, which sat on his muscular unaccustomed limbs like plate armour, and a conspicuously white shirt, his face shining at once with friction and devotion. There was a sober radiance, and yet a sense of responsibility about his countenance which continually attracted me to it, and I always found myself ending my survey of my neighbours with that dear reverent old face, as if unconsciously I recognised it to be a shrine and altar from which more than could be heard or seen was going up to heaven.

And it must be confessed that there was much to distract my attention. If the wages-paying and wages-receiving classes were thus sharply defined by the material of their clothes, the minor distinctions among their richer neighbours were equally marked to a discriminating eye by their chronology. It was but at a slow pace that our town toilettes could approach the standard of the Squire's, and still further of the Countess' pew, in those brief intervals when the Countess shone on us.

Many decades of the fashion-book were thus represented around me, and it was impossible that my eye should not be arrested by varieties reaching from the aristocratic French classics of tight skirts and short waists, to the hoop and high whalebone hood of Miss Felicity Benbow, the schoolmistress, to whom a Sunday dress was a possession for life, and who would as soon have thought of changing her grandfather the general's Tory principles for Jacobinism, as her mother's fashions for raiment, which she severely, but blushingly, characterized as "little better than none at all."

I was not conscious of doing anything profane or un-sabbatical in thus contemplating my neighbours.

At that time no gorgeous varieties of symbolical vesture had been thought of for the clergy; but I had no doubt that these varieties of costume among the laity formed as integral a part of the Sunday festivities as Tate and Brady, Reuben Pengelly's great bass-viol, and my uncle Parson Fyford's preaching a sermon in the pulpit robed in black.

I cannot remember anything special in those sermons; but I do remember well waking up from time to time, not as far as I know by external suggestions, to a sense of meaning and a sense of appropriation in various parts of the Liturgy.

First there was the Lord's Prayer. Whatever else in the service might be the peculiar possession of grown-up people, that plainly belonged to us children. We said it every morning and evening. Then there was the Apostles' Creed, which seemed to belong to the Lord's Prayer, beginning with the Almighty Father and going on with its simple history of the Saviour who came from heaven, who also like us had once a mother, and was nailed on the dreadful cross, and had died and had been "buried" like our mother; but unlike her, had risen again. He had, I knew, made other people rise again, but not mother yet. But one day He would make us all rise again; for that, father had told me, was what the end of the Creed meant. And then I should see Mother.

But there were two versicles in the Prayer-Book which, being entirely incomprehensible to me, I always privately revised.

Whatever the rest of the congregation might be able to say, being grown up, and no doubt having better consciences than I had, I, ignorant of archaic English, and keenly conscious of my own misdoings, could certainly never pray that God would "not deal with me after my sins," and " would not reward me after my iniquities." I who had become entangled in such a bewildering labyrinth of sins and iniquities, could I ask God not to deal any more after them with me? Therefore I always left out the "not." "Not dealing with me," as I understood it, so exactly represented my stepmother's mode of punishment. My

food was given me, lessons were taught me,
all the mechanism of life went on, even to
the morning and evening kiss; but I, as a
little, trembling, clinging, living, loving
personality, was left out, ignored, the
averted eye never meeting mine, my words
indeed answered; my wants supplied, but I
myself unresponded to altogether; close in
body, in heart and soul banished into outer
darkness. I myself was simply "not dealt
with."

If God were at all like that, watching
coldly and gravely in the expectation I
should go wrong; what a destiny, if for
ever and ever I were to live in his sight
and within his hearing, under the icy
weight of his cold displeasure, not clear why
I had offended Him, and feeling it quite
hopeless to ask, without the resource even of
an occasional flash of indignant revolt, because of course He must be right !

Those versicles are, however, especially

memorable to me as connected with one
especial Sunday afternoon.

I had gone through a week of those small
misdemeanours and misfortunes, connected,
as usual, chiefly with behaviour and clothes,
in which mischance and misdoing were so
inextricably confused to me, yet in which I
so often felt that if the original offence
which had drawn down the displeasure of
my stepmother had been trifling, the burning anger and revolt aroused in me were *not*
trifles. Moreover, I had fallen into two
undeniable passions about wrongs done, as I
conceived, to Piers, and to the reigning
kitten.

That Sunday, therefore, with unusual fer-
vour, and with bitter secret tears, I had prayed
my little private revision of the Liturgy.

"Deal with me! oh do not give up dealing with me after my sins."

Poor blundering childish prayer, I believe
it was heard.

I had certainly no irreverent intention of correcting the compilers of the Prayer-Book, I only thought I must be so much worse than other people who could calmly say the words as they were printed! Otherwise, of course the words would never have been there. My stepmother had so often told me I was quite exceptionally naughty, and this Sunday at least, after such a week, I felt it must be true; more especially because my father himself, having come in at the climax of one of my passions, and not knowing the cause, had looked gravely distressed at me.

That Sunday afternoon it happened that my father was occupied with visitors, and Piers and I crept away to our usual resource, through the field to the Foundry-yard, to pay a visit to Reuben Pengelly and Prisey his wife. They lived at the gate-house, and we were welcomed as usual. But I was very unhappy, feeling like a

little exile even there. While Piers was
sitting complacently on old Priscy Pengelly's knee, enjoying her adoration and
his bit of apple pasty, I, quite beyond
the consolation of caresses and pasties,
sate and nursed my sorrows on the little
wooden stool in the porch at Reuben's
feet.

The very quiet of the place seemed to
irritate me. I had so many hammers beat-
ing, and complicated wheels revolving in my
little heart and brain, that the usual din
and rattle of the works would have been
more congenial to me.

Everything but me was so good and
quiet and fit for Sunday! The water playing over the idle wheel, the lazy occasional
creaking of some of the machinery (like a
yawn of Pluto awakened out of sleep), the
quiet noiseless investigations being pursued
by Priscy's cat among heaps of iron, and
stationary machines she would not have

dared to come near on work-days; the absence of all the clamorous busy life that filled the place at other times, and the peace and shining cleanliness of Reuben's house and face, always made that porch seem to me the most Sunday-like place in the world. And I liked to hear old Reuben and Priscy talk, in a way I only half understood, but always, I felt, in good kind voices, about good and happy things.

But that day the disquiet within was too deep to be soothed by the quiet without.

All Reuben's benevolent attempts to draw me into happy childish talk had failed, and at length, Piers having fallen asleep on Priscy's knee, and Priscy having fallen fast asleep too, Reuben looked tenderly down at me, and seeing, I suppose, the dull, stony look so unnatural on a childish face, he said—

"My lamb, what makes thee so wisht?"

It happened that just then I was watching a little drama being enacted on the opposite

side of the yard, between Priscy's cat and a
large brown hen. Anxiously the poor
mother, ignorant of the restraints imposed
on pussy by our presence, had been calling
her chickens to her, and at length had succeeded in attracting the last of them from
the seductions of crumbs and grains under
the shelter of her wings. And there she
sat tenderly clucking over her little ones,
nestled close to her ; and heroically confront-
ing the enemy.

I had watched the little parable with a
strange, choking bitterness ; and, at first,
when Reuben spoke I could say nothing.

But, when he stooped down and stood me
beside his knee, and then took me on it and
held my hands so tenderly in his great sinewy
hand, the first ice-crust of my reserve began
to melt, and I said quietly—I felt too des-
pairing for tears—

"Reuben, I cannot be good. I *cannot*. I
have done so many sins and iniquities. I

think God is going to give up dealing with me."

I suppose he thought my case not very hopeless, for he smiled most complacently and said—

" Give thee up, poor lamb! *At last!* Why He did not give up dealing with *me!*"

I did not feel the force of the consolation. What could Reuben have done as naughty as I had? I only shook my head.

" Why, what be ye thinking about, Miss Bride, my dear?" came out in his hearty voice. " The Lord is good, *good;* with poor, hardened old sinners, and to thee! an innocent babe like thee!"

I felt much more like a hardened sinner whatever that meant, than like an innocent babe; and suddenly something that had lain hidden at the bottom of my heart rose up at his words—something I could never have said to father, and had scarcely *said* even to myself.

"Reuben," I said, looking straight up into his eyes, " *is* God good ? To you, Reuben. But not to me ; not to me. He took away Mother ! Even those little chickens have somewhere warm and soft to hide ; and I have nowhere. God took away Mother from me. He must have known I should never be good afterwards. He is *not* good to me."

Happily for me, the old man did not crush the helpless cry of anguish with a reproof, as if it had been a mere wilful cry of revolt. But a look of pain came over his face, such as I should have felt if Piers had struck father ! And he said, looking reverently upwards—

"Poor lamb ! Poor motherless babe ! She knows not what she says. She wants to be good ; and she doesn't know how. Thou want'st !—Thou who hast died for it !"

"I do want to be good, Reuben," I said, afraid I had not been quite honest; "but I want—oh I want *Mother !*"

"My lamb, my lamb," he said, " you want God! Mother is happy, for she loves God. She did when she was here, dear soul, and now she is with him and loves him better; for she knows how God loves."

" *Is* Mother happy, Reuben?" I said, roused to an unwonted daring. "How can she be happy? If she is living and awake, how can she be happy, and I so unhappy, and not good, and never going to be good? Why even I could not be happy, on Father's knee, and Father pleased with me, if Piers were hurt or naughty. And how could Mother? She loved us more than that. I know, I know, if God would let her, Mother would come back from anywhere—from *anywhere*, to help us and make us good. It is God who took her away, and will not ever let her come back. And how can I pretend to love God or say that He is good to me?"

Reuben said nothing, but kept stroking my hands. I was afraid he was vexed. But when I glanced up at him I thought he had never looked so kind, although great tears were on his cheeks.

And then gently, as if I had been an infant, he carried me into his little house, and shut the door, and knelt down, with me beside him, and prayed till the drops stood on his forehead and the tears rained down his face.

He said something like this :—

" O, blessed Father ! Pity this poor wisht, forlorn babe. She has lost her mother, and she has lost sight of Thee. She doesn't understand. She thinks Thou art turning away Thy face from her, and not caring for her. And all the time it is Thou who art stooping down, and likening Thyself to *anything*, to that poor helpless fool of a hen gathering her chickens, just to make us understand how Thou lovest us—calling, calling, spreading out Thy wings—for her, for her ! Lord, make the little one understand ; make the babe hear and see.

"Blessed Lord Jesus, Thou knowest how we want to hear and touch and see; above all, the little ones. Thou camest that we might touch and see. Thou tookest them in Thine arms, and laid Thine hands on them, that they might touch and see. Thou hast let them nail Thee to the Cross that we might feel and see. Ah, good Shepherd! and this little lamb has lost sight of thee altogether! But Thou hearest her crying. Lord, it's only the lamb bleating for its mother—Thy little lamb bleating for Thee! Take her home on Thy shoulders, Lord. Take her home to Thy heart, and make her happy and make her good."

Then he rose and sat down, and took me on his knees again. I leant my head on his shoulder, and was quite quiet—quiet in my heart too.

"My lamb," he said, "that's it; that's all. You want God. And God wants you to be good. He gave his own Son for us. He would have left mother with you if he could. 'Seems to me He wants you just to look up, as it were, and see mother smiling on you in heaven, *as sure enough she is,* and then turning round to Him, *just that you may follow her eyes,* and turn round to Him too, and see how He is smiling on her, and on you both. Child, child! mother *is* happy! And she would never be happy unless she knew God was good, and good to you. Follow her looks up to His face my lamb, and you will see what she sees."

All the time I had not cried. I had felt too naughty and wretched. But those words went to my heart.

"Mother knows God is good, *and good to me.*"

And I did try to follow her looks upwards to His face.

And He helped me; He did not give up dealing with me.

My new treasure was soon tested. For

I remember the very evening after that Sunday afternoon talk with Reuben had begun to clear things a little to me, I ventured to say to my stepmother when I kissed her for the night, that I really hoped now I should be good, for I thought I had a little love to God, and he would help me.

My heart was glowing, yet it cost me much to stammer out those words. To me it was like a confession. It was in the Oak Parlour. She was looking out of the window. She turned round a little surprised, and questioned me with her eyes till I turned crimson; but she only said—

"Very well, Bridget. I am sure I hope you will be good. You are liable to very violent ebullitions of feeling. I think it was two days since you called me cruel because your kitten was whipped for stealing cream, and three days since you tried to take up your brother and kiss him when he was naughty and was put in the corner, and threw yourself into a frantic rage with me because I would not let you, which your father saw; and four days since you sat sobbing half an hour as if your heart would break, because you had torn your pinafore, and had to mend it, instead of playing in the garden. You are subject to very vehement changes of emotion. I suppose this is one of them. I hope it will last, and that you will in future wash your hands in time for dinner, and keep your hair smooth. *I* judge by fruits."

I crept humbled away, with the feeling one has in seeing the dog in Landseer's picture, with wistful eyes and appealing paws, entreating the parrot for a crumb of cheese.

Yet I believe the hail-showers and glaciers of my childhood were good for me, as well as its sunshine and soft dews. I went away saddened, but no more chilled to the heart; for I had learned that the sunshine and the dews, and soft brooding warm wings of ever present love were at least as real as the cold. The key was in my hand; it has never been quite lost since; and secret after secret is unlocked to me whenever I touch the doors of hidden chambers with it.

So, as it happened, my feeling after mother became at last a feeling after God, and finding Him, which, I suppose, was part at least of what He meant.

It was on the Sunday after this that I was thinking I wished mother had been among some " goodly fellowship " or " glorious company" or " noble army" mentioned in the *Te Deum*, that I might be sure she was among those we sang about as praising with us. And then it occurred to me that the Holy Church throughout the world could not mean the little bit of it where we are and which we see; where the prophets and apostles are not any longer.

I remembered Reuben's words, and all at

once a heavy roof seemed lifted off from the world, and I followed Mother's eyes up to His face, and saw that the Church of our old town was only a little corner of the great Church throughout the world which is always praising Him ; and that I, down in the dark room, and Mother up in the light where she was waiting for me, without anything between, were singing our *Te Deum* together.

Thus the service gradually grew to shine out on me, bit by bit, like far-off fields on our own moors lighted up one by one by the sun.

My attention to the sermon was less-endangered by external objects ; for I was always caused during its delivery to subside into the depths of a great pew, above whose walls nothing was visible to me but my uncle, Parson Fyford, the top of Miss Felicity's whalebone hood, the bows in Madam Glanvil's bonnet, which used periodically to sway about and disappear, and then to re-

cover and erect themselves inexplicably, in
a defiant manner; the grave face of Reuben
Pengelly above the choir gallery, and the
trees waving in the churchyard outside the
windows.

I remember wondering why my Uncle
Fyford put on quite a different voice from
that in which he spoke to us during the
week, and whether I should ever be expected
to understand what he said.

But my most vivid recollections of the
sermon, especially after that Sunday afternoon with Reuben in the Foundry-yard, were
of a time of delicious rest, when the two
people who were kindest to me in the world
were looking down serenely on me, and Piers
being, by father's express sanction, allowed
to go to sleep, was leaning his sleepy little
head against me, and I was feeling like a
little mother to him, with one hand around
him, and the other nestled in father's; whilst
above us was the dear sacred name on a

white marble tablet, and a consciousness of a
sacred corner outside in the churchyard, and
of something more sacred and tenderer still
above us in the sky; a light deeper than the
sunlight, a smile kinder than father's, embracing mother and us, all.

And eager and restless as I was, the sermon did not seem long to me; and a heaven
" where congregations ne'er break up,"
would not have seemed to me a terrible
threat at all.

CHAPTER VI.

AN excess of theology was not the excess prevalent in Abbot's Weir in my childhood. "High" and "low" in those days had reference rather to social than to ecclesiastical elevations; and "broad" was applied to acres or to cloth, not to opinions.

Whatever purposes the laity went to church for, severe critical analysis of my uncle Fyford's or his curate's sermons was not one of them.

I remember not unfrequently hearing strong comments on the extravagance of some people's garments and the imperfections of others', but never any derogatory remarks on the extravagances or defects, or "unsoundness" of any kind, of the various doctrines delivered to us.

Occasionally I recollect my father's gently protesting that the Doctor—my uncle was a D.D.—had "given us that again a little too soon;" but a suspicion that sermons were intended to be transferred beyond the church doors for discussion (or, I am afraid also, for practice), never crossed my mind.

Indeed, all the sects represented in our little town had subsided into a state of mutual tolerance which might have seemed exemplary, had not this tolerance extended to some things which all Christian sects are not supposed to tolerate.

Protests were not the style of the day. "Against the stream" scarcely any one seemed pulling. The effect was a drowsy tranquillity. The various pulpits would as little have ventured to fulminate against the enormities of the slave-trade, the intoxication common at all convivial gatherings, the

rioting at the races on our Down, the
cruelties of our bull-baitings in the market-
place, as against each other.

"Were the feelings of the congregation
to be wantonly disregarded?" my uncle
Fyford would have pleaded. "Had not
one of Madame Glanvil's sons been a slave-
holder? and had not the enormities of the
slave-trade been greatly exaggerated? Were
there any of the most respectable of the
congregation who did not occasionally take
a glass too much?" (drunkenness was not
then a mere low habit of the "lower
classes;") "and were the little 'harmless
frailties' of the 'most respectable' of the
parishioners to be wantonly dragged into
the light? And even the 'lower orders,'
no doubt, must also have their amusements;
poor creatures, their lot of toil was hard
enough already without being further em-
bittered by Puritanical austerities. What
was the occasional discomfort of a bull, a

creature without a soul (and without a literature to celebrate its wrongs), compared with the importance of keeping up a manly, ancient English pastime, a healthy outlet, no doubt, for a certain—brutality,—we will not call it, but—a certain recklessness of blood inherent in the very vigour of the Saxon nature? Was there not even a text for it? Had not St. Paul said (possibly not in precisely the same connection), 'Did God take care for oxen?' And should we be more merciful than St. Paul? No; let such pretences be left to the over-refined sensibilities of a Jean Jacques Rousseau, to a nation which could guillotine its sovereign and weep over a sentimental love-story (especially if the love were misplaced), or to the gloomy asceticism of an austere Puritanism, now, happily for England, extinct."

I used sometimes to suspect from the vehemence with which my uncle defended this custom, he being at once a tranquil and a merciful man, that his conscience was a little uneasy at the sufferings to which, as a devoted entomologist, he exposed the various beetles which were impaled in the glass cases in the vicarage. He could always be roused on the subject of the nervous sensibilities of animals, and I remember a hot debate between him and my father on Shakspere's lines :—

> " The beetle that we tread upon
> In corporal sufferance feels a pang as keen
> As when a giant dies,—"

which my uncle characterized as sentimental and pernicious trash.

I believe he would very gladly have stretched the same conviction to the nervous sensibilities of negroes; but his candour was too much for him; and with regard to the abolition of the slave-trade he had to take up other grounds, such as the general tendency of Africans to make each other miserable in Africa, if let alone, and the antecedent improbability that "Providence" would have created a substance so attractive to white people as sugar, and so impossible for white people to cultivate, and would have prospered our sugar plantations and sugar planters as It had, unless It had meant that sugar should be cultivated by blacks, and consequently that blacks should be brought from Africa.

Thus it happened, in consequence of all these various arguments, or rather in consequence of the prepossessions by which so many of our arguments are predetermined, that Abbot's Weir protested against very little, at that time, either in church or chapel. My uncle did indeed periodically protest against various evils mostly remote or obsolete, such as Popery on the anniversary of the Gunpowder Plot, the heresies of the fourth century on Trinity Sunday, or the schisms of the seventeenth century on the festival of King Charles the Martyr.

But he rejoiced to think that we had fallen on different times, when Englishmen had learned to live in harmony.

Did not he himself indeed exemplify this harmony by a cordial if somewhat condescending intercourse with the Rev. Josiah Rabbidge, the mild successor of the fiery Cromwellian minister who, at the Restoration, had been driven from the pulpit of the parish church ?

Mild indeed had that Presbyterian congregation become, in doctrine, in discipline, and in zeal ; and difficult would it have been for any one short of a Spanish Inquisitor of the keenest scent to fasten a quarrel on theological grounds on the Rev. Josiah Rabbidge, a gentle and shy little man whose personality was all but overwhelmed under the combined weight of a tall and aggressive wife, the fourteen children with which she had enriched him, the instruction of the boys of the town when they emerged from the mixed Dame's School of Miss Felicity Benbow, and a congregation which it was not easy to keep awake, especially on Sunday afternoons.

On this last fact I had personal experience, one of our maids being sometimes in the habit of taking us to the chapel on Sunday afternoons, when Uncle Fyford was preaching in his second church in the country; attracted, I believe, not by the theology, but by the greater brevity of the service, and the greater comfort of the cushions.

I do not remember being struck with any great difference, except that Mr. Rabbidge's prayers were shorter, and not in the Prayer-Book, and that he generally used the term "the Deity" where my uncle said "Providence."

I suppose the terms were characteristic in both cases. Mr. Rabbidge's element, when he could escape to it, was literature; my uncle's, nature. To both human life was a subordinate thing. To my uncle, indeed, it was brought near by the household presence of his orphan nephew, Dick Fyford, and three thousand parishioners, who had at intervals to be married, christened, and buried; and to Mr. Rabbidge by the constant inevitable pressure of a wife to be propitiated, fourteen children to be fed, a large portion of the boy-humanity of Abbot's Weir to be taught, and that somnolent congregation to be kept awake. Still to both all this tide of human life was a disturbing accident, from which they escaped when practicable — Mr. Rabbidge to his dearly-prized ancient folios, and my uncle to his beetles. And as must happen, I think, to all from whom the human life around recedes, the Divine seemed to recede also; and on the very pursuits they cared for more than for humanity fell a lifelessness and a barrenness. Nature herself re-

fuses to be more than a scientific catalogue
to those who subordinate humanity to her.
The thoughts and lives of the men of the
past become mere fossils to those who neglect for them the living men and women of
the present. If the present does not live
for us, how can the past? If our "neighbour" has no personality we reverence and
supremely care for, how can nature be to
us more than a collection of things? If
humanity does not come home to our hearts,
how can God? Thus, in a measure, mode-
rated indeed by the merciful duties they
were inclined to look on as hindrances, the
law of love avenged itself. Nature became
to my uncle not so much a living wonder
and glory, as a storehouse to furnish glass-
cases for insects; and history to Mr. Rabbidge rather a museum of antiquities than
a record of continuous life; and God not so
much the Father and the Saviour as the
" Providence " which arranges with mar-

vellous ingenuity the mechanism of the universe, or "the Deity" which dwells afar off in thick darkness at the sources of History.

Of the Incarnation, or of the Cross, they had little need, in such a view of nature and of human life.

It was probably, therefore, rather by an accident of position that my uncle retained the dogma in his creed, whilst Mr. Rabbidge had glided, unperceived by his congregation, and possibly by himself, into a mild and most unaggressive Arianism.

And yet in all this I speak rather of their theories, and of what these would have made them, than of themselves; or rather of what they would have made themselves than of what God made them.

My uncle could not, with the best intentions, live for beetles, nor Mr. Rabbidge for books.

That rollicking cousin of ours, Dick

Fyford, was perpetually plucking him back
to the roughest realities of human life in its
crudest form of British Boy; to the crudest
form of British Boy, a boy with an in-
vincible inclination for the sea.

And to poor Mr. Rabbidge's discipline,
no doubt, all Abbot's Weir contributed,
from Mrs. Rabbidge to Piers and Dick
Fyford, as Mrs. Danescombe did to mine.
What fossils, what monsters, or what intolerable bores we should become if we
could get rid of the things and persons in
our lives we are apt to call hindrances!

The intercourse between my uncle and
Mr. Rabbidge was, no doubt, made more
amicable by the manifest differences in their
persons and positions. There could, my
uncle felt, be no danger of a man forgetting
the social distinctions caused by the union
of Church and State, who had, to begin
with, to raise his eyes eighteen inches
before they encountered his own, whose

rapid, hesitating utterance contrasted cha-
racteristically with my uncle's slow, round,
sonorous enunciation; who had to compress
sixteen people into the Old Abbey Gate-
house, an appendage of the rectory for
which my uncle declined to receive any but
a peppercorn rent; to whom the glebe cows
and vegetables were as serviceable as to the
rector himself.

Not that Mr. Rabbidge's independence of
thought was in any way affected by these
favours, or by the necessity of accepting
them. No sense of favours past or to come
would have made him indifferent to the
value of a Greek particle, not, I mean, only
in the Athanasian Creed, but anywhere;
and he had heresies from the Oxford pronunciation of Greek and Latin, in defence
of which he would have suffered any persecution, civil or domestic. In this the spirit
of his Puritan ancestors survived in him,
and not even the eloquent and forcible Mrs.

Rabbidge herself could have constrained him to any compliance beyond silence.

But my uncle's sense of ecclesiastical dignity was satisfied by conferring these benefits. It was not necessary by any extra chill and polish of manner further to accentuate a difference already sufficiently marked. And therefore the intercourse was of the friendliest kind, Mr. Rabbidge's fourteen were welcome at all times to enter the rectory garden through the arched door, which connected it with the little garden of the Gatehouse, Dick Fyford being after all a far more dangerous inmate than the whole fourteen together.

Meanwhile Mr. Rabbidge found recondite allusions to beetles in the classics, Greek and Latin, and my uncle returned the compliment by referring in his articles in the *Sentimental Magazine* to quotations suggested by his "learned friend, Mr. Rabbidge." One point my uncle never yielded

to "separatists." As an orthodox Church-
man, and as the minister of a State religion,
he could not be expected to concede to the
alumnus of a Dissenting academy the title
of Reverend. It would, he considered, be
to eliminate all significance from the word.
"Titles," said my uncle, "*are* titles; to
accord the right to confer them on any self-
elected community is to undermine the
citadel of all authority. Persons who began by calling a Presbyterian teacher Reverend, might naturally end with calling their
sovereign 'citizen.' Mr. Rabbidge would,
he knew, comprehend his motives." And
Mr. Rabbidge did, and never protested.

For they had the link said to be stronger
than a common love—a common hate; if so
fiery a word may be applied to any sentiment possible in zones so temperate.

They both hated "Jacobinism"—my
uncle as a man of property, which any convulsions might endanger, and Mr. Rabbidge

as a peaceable and not very valiant citizen,
who in any contest was not likely to get the
upper hand.

And they both disapproved of Methodism,
the only aggressive form of religion they were
acquainted with—my uncle condemning it
chiefly as having a "Jacobinical" tendency
to set up the "lower orders" and to "turn
the world upside down," and Mr. Rabbidge
as an enthusiasm likely to set people's
hearts above their heads, and so turn their
brains upside down.

And yet, such are the inconsistencies of
the best balanced minds, Reuben Pengelly
continued every Sunday morning to play
the principal bass-viol in the choir gallery,
every Sunday evening to take a principal
part in the prayers and exhortations in the
little Methodist meeting, and every day and
night, everywhere when he was wanted, to
pray beside the dying beds or broken hearts
among my uncle's parishioners.

And there were instances in which Mr. Rabbidge had even been known to call poor Reuben in, when he had found his somnolent and respectable congregation roused by some dim memory of the old Puritan teaching, for which their forefathers had fought, or by some of the terrible realities of life or death, to an unquenchable thirst for something which he did not comprehend, which neither the mild Arianism of the chapel, nor the mild orthodoxy of the church afforded, but which Reuben seemed able to give; some dim orphaned feeling after One who is more than "Providence" and "the Deity," whom Reuben trusted and called on, in no very classical English, "the Lord, the living Lord, the Lord who died for us and liveth evermore, the loving, pitying, and providing God and Father of us all."

My uncle and Mr. Rabbidge both thought it very strange; but human nature, especially in the "lower orders" and in women, is a strange compound; what classical author has not in one phrase or another said so?

Principle, sober principle, the incontrovertible precepts of morality, ought to be enough for rational humanity; but in all the relations of life, and even it seemed in religion, men and women, especially women, could not be satisfied without something more than sober principle to guide their judgment; they must have their hearts stirred, they must laugh for joy, and tremble, and weep—they must have emotion; and as this was so, perhaps it was well that a man, on the whole so respectful to authority and so trustworthy as Reuben Pengelly, was to be found to supply the material.

Or as Reuben put it:—

"The devil took care there should always be sinners, and the Lord took care there should always be saints beyond the reach of anything but his blessed Gospel and his good Spirit."

CHAPTER VII

OPPOSITE our windows, across the Corn Market, was a long, low, rambling old house, once a dower house of the Glanvil family, but long before my recollection the abode of Miss Felicity Benbow, the guide and the terror of successive generations of juvenile Abbot's Weir.

Piers and I, sitting on the window-seat of the Stone Parlour, frequently observed the children going in and out of that wide arched door. The house and Miss Felicity herself had a kind of horrible fascination for us. Sooner or later, we knew those solemn portals would open on us, and ingulf us also in that unknown world within, where dwelt the dark shadowy powers of discipline and knowledge represented in the person of Miss Felicity.

Thither every morning and afternoon we saw the children, a little older than ourselves—some, it was rumoured, *not* older—tend in twos or threes, or one by one, with lingering and sober steps, the small satchel on the shoulder, and occasionally the book too late consulted being anxiously conned over; and thence, in a body at the appointed hour, we saw them issue with softened voices and quiet sobered paces for a few steps beyond the door, as far, at least, as the range of Miss Felicity's windows, subdued by the restraints of those unknown powers within; and then through the narrow streets, in different directions, we heard the joyous voices sound louder and freer as they distanced the solemn precincts, scattering frolic and music through the town as they separated to their different homes.

There, also, on wet days the various

maids of the richer families gathered with
hoods and cloaks for their young masters
and mistresses. And there every morning
and evening the aristocrat of the school,
Madam Glanvil's little orphan granddaughter, was brought and fetched, by the
old black butler in livery, on her white
pony; a grave, retiring child with dark,
pallid complexion and overhanging brows,
and with large, wistful brown eyes, which
often seemed to meet mine, and always
seemed to speak to me from some mysterious new world. The rest of the children
thought her proud and supercilious, but
those strange, deep eyes with their wonderful occasional lights, not the dewy sparkle
of English eyes, but a flash as from tropical
skies, always had an irresistible attraction
for me. They had a wistful longing in them
like Pluto's eyes, and yet a depth I could
not fathom, which always drew me back
questioning and guessing. Something be-

tween the mysteries of the dumb animal world and the mysteries of the invisible spirit-world was in them. I could not tell why; but they made me think at once of the dog Pluto, and of my mother.

I could watch no one whilst she was there, and I grew to feel at last that the attraction must be mutual, for she always guided the white pony near our windows, and in a furtive way used, I felt, to watch Piers and me, although she always looked away if our eyes met. Occasionally, moreover, on stormy days, an old black nurse used to appear, with two black footmen and a sedan-chair, instead of the one negro with the white pony. The black nurse used to apparel the young lady in a mass of orange and scarlet splendours, and enter the chair with her, and then in stately procession Miss Amice Glanvil would be borne away to the fine old manor-house among the woods on the hill, called Court.

Altogether, therefore, Miss Amice was to me like a tropical dream of glow and gloom, such as our temperate zone could not produce; a creature from a region of splendours and shadows, altogether deeper and richer than ours; a region where the birds and flowers are scarlet and gold; a land of earthquakes and hurricanes, and wildernesses of beauty, of magnificence, and tragedy.

For I knew that those black people were slaves, and the gleam of their white teeth, and the flash of their brilliant eyes when they pulled their woolly locks, as they used goodhumouredly to do to us children watching at the window, used not to terrify me as it did many of the children in the town, nor to amuse me; but to make me feel inclined to cry. They always made me think of Pluto when he was chained up in the kennel and fawned and whined on us. Only Pluto was at home, and they were

not; and Pluto was a dog, and they were
not; which made all the difference, I
thought, for him and for them. They were
called also by the classical names which in
France and in Italy have retained their
dignity, but in England were only given in
a sort of kindly contempt or facetious pity
to dogs and to negroes. I had heard the
black woman call them Cato and Cæsar;
and they called her Chloe.

Moreover we had, through Reuben Pengelly, an acquaintance with Chloe's history
which gave us a glimpse into the tragedy
which underlaid the splendours of Amice
Glanvil's life.

Chloe had a whole woman's world of her
own, in her own country in Africa; not
dead; living still and needing her still; but
buried to her irrevocably and for ever.

She used to come now and then, when she
was allowed, to Reuben's prayer-meetings,
and sometimes rather to confuse him by

the fervency of her Amens, and of her
shrill quavering singing, in the refrains of
the hymns. One evening she still further
bewildered the kindly man by breaking out
suddenly in a passion of sobs.

Reuben told us the story on the next
Sunday, in the silent Foundry-yard.

"I couldn't for the life of me tell why,"
he said, he having no oratorical vanity to
explain such emotion. "I was only talking
to the folks quite plain and quiet how the
blessed Lord sate weary by the well, and
asked the poor woman for a drink from her
pitcher, and how she was slow to give it
Him. Chloe stayed after the rest had gone,
still rocking herself to and fro, as if she
were rocking a baby, hiding her face, and
sobbing fit to break her heart. So I went
up to her soft and quiet, not to fluster her,
and I said, 'The Lord has touched thee,
poor dear soul. Cheer up. He wounds
and He can bind up.' 'Never, Massa

Reuben, *never,*' said she (poor soul, she
always calls me Massa, she knows no
better). 'Never bind up. *He knows better
than to try.* Let the wounds bleed. No
other way.' And then, in their sudden
way, like children, she looked up and
showed all her white teeth, and smiled, and
downright laughed. It was more than a
man could make out. 'It was all along of
that pitcher and that well,' said she. And
then she told how she had gone to the well
one evening, years ago, by her hut, away in
Africa, with her pitcher, to fetch water for
her children, with her baby in her arms.
The children lay sick with fever. But at
the well the slave-hunters found her,
gagged her, bound her, forced her away to
the coast, and squeezed her down with
hundreds of others into the slave-ship.
She heard the sick children, day and night,
moaning—moaning for her. Many of the
poor creatures with her refused to eat, and

many died; but she had the baby, and tried
to live. And as she went on telling she
cried again, and then she smiled again.
'Never mind me, Massa Reuben,' said she;
'it was only that pitcher. Seemed to me
all the place, and all the years melted away.
I was at home again at that well again with
the pitcher, and instead of the slave-hunters
the good Lord Himself stood there, and
said, "Give me to drink." And she seemed
to answer Him her pitcher was gone, all
was gone, she had nothing to draw with,
and there was nothing to draw. And He
said, all smiling, it was not the water He
wanted, but just herself. 'Just me,' said
she, 'sitting there weary, just as He did
once, poor old Chloe, that He died for; me
and my bit of love.' And she saw the
hands and the feet all torn and bleeding,
worse than dust on them that a woman's
tears might wash away, blood on them to
wash away her sins, and she seemed just to

take her heart, as it was all dry and empty, and give it Him. 'And He looked as glad,' said she, 'as a thirsty man for a drink of water. All for me, Massa Reuben, all because He cared to be loved by me!'" And then Reuben said, "I cried too, just as she did, poor soul ! Her baby had died just as the voyage was over, and then when they came on shore Squire Glanvil bought her for a nurse to Miss Amice. His wife had just died at her birth, and the poor fool loves Miss Amice like her own. Its wonderful," concluded Reuben, " what them poor creatures will cling to and catch at, just for anything to love, though for the matter of that, Priscy's no better. The women are like enough all the world over, poor souls. God bless them ! "

Miss Felicity used sometimes to descend to the door with the little lady, and watch her across the market-place, which gave us

ample opportunity of studying that physi-
ognomy so important to our future fate.

She was a tall and rather a majestic
woman, with a stiff erect carriage (a
perpetual monition to all lounging little
boys and girls), keen black eyes, high
Roman features, and a severe mouth resolutely closed, as if her life had been a
battle with difficulties harder to conquer
than the little mischievous elves who could
never evade her penetrating eyes, or the
terrible instrument of justice they guided.

Yet it was not a face which repelled me,
or made me feel afraid. I felt rather drawn
towards her, as a kind of tutelary Athena;
not very close, not exactly as a child to her
heart, but as a subject to her feet, with a
kind of confidence of justice in those steady
eyes, and those stern grave lips. There
was no fretfulness in the lines of the
furrowed brow, or in the curve of the
mouth; no uncertainty of temper in the

large keen eyes. If she had carried the
Ægis, I do not think I should have had any
fear of her petrifying the wrong people by
turning it on them.

There were two other inhabitants of that
old mansion besides Miss Felicity.

Every fine morning in summer, before
people were up, and every fine evening in
winter as it began to grow dusk, from that
arched door, where poured in and out every
day the joyous tide of young life, came
forth two very different figures, one the
stately form of Miss Felicity, and the other
a man tall as herself, but bowed and stooping, moving with uncertain and uneven
gait, and leaning on Miss Felicity's arm.
They crept away into the country by the
least steep of the three roads which led out
of the town, and in about an hour re-
entered the old house and disappeared, and
the stooping tall man's figure was seen no
more till next day. It was believed they

went always as far as a certain ancient well by the roadside called the Benit or Blessed Well; for they were often seen resting on the stone bench beside it, and had never been found farther on.

It was curious how people respected the mystery Miss Felicity chose to consider thrown around that ruined life. Keen as her perceptions were, sharp and definite her words on every other subject, around him she gathered a veil of fond excuses and illusions, so thin that all the town saw through it, and yet all the town recognised it for her sake.

To us children indeed something of the mystery really existed, taking the form of a half-concealing, half-glorifying mist which surrounded Miss Felicity with a halo, and through which the tall, bent form loomed. at once a tower and a beacon, like a ruined church set on one of the heights along our coasts, once meant to be a sacred shrine, but now, the sacredness shattered out of it, surviving only as a warning against wreck.

Lieutenant Benbow had been in the army, we knew, and had been a fine handsome man, and had grown suddenly old in middle life, not altogether by misfortune, but by something sadder, which hung like a sword of Damocles over the festival of life for any of us to whom life was only feasting.

To me especially those two had a terrible yet tender interest.

Lieutenant Benbow had been to Miss Felicity what Piers was to me. She had loved him, delighted in him, lived for him after the death of her father. (Happily for herself the mother had died early.) She had loved him with the kind of blind love which some think the truest and most womanly. To me the blindness always seems to come not from the love, but from the little alloy of pride and selfishness in the love which so far makes it false. It is possible so to love another as ourselves, that the very love comes to partake of the nature of self-love, exaggerating, concealing, untrue, unjust, falsely excusing, falsely gilding. And yet, not quite. The little grain of true love at the bottom of the most selfish affection, makes it by that grain at least better than mere selfishness. The miser who half starves his children in hoarding for them has surely in his hoard something a degree more sacred than there can be in that of the miser who hoards for himself alone. And with Miss Felicity that grain of true love was large, and for herself at least, fruitful; fruitful at least in sacrifice.

Lieutenant Benbow had followed his father's profession. Their means were not large; but her delight had been to have his appointments as choice and abundant as those of the richest. And the idol had

accepted the homage, repaid it even by
such small and symbolical acknowledg-
ments as can be expected from duly in-
censed idols.

She knew he had at least one fatal habit.
In a day when all gentlemen drank more
than was good for them, he drank more
than most, and unfortunately could stand
less.

Once only Miss Felicity's eyes were all
but opened. He persuaded a lovely young
Quaker girl to elope with him and to marry
him.

Miss Felicity did not wonder at the
Quaker maiden's infatuation; but she did
wonder at her brother's. The Quaker
maiden's father was a tanner, and, true
daughter of a general and of the Church,
granddaughter of a bishop, Miss Felicity
did not enjoy having to double her libations
and incense in honour, not of her Adonis
of a brother, but of his separatist wife, a

person of " low trading origin who had
enticed away his affections." To double
her offerings and lose even the little return
they had previously won was almost too
much to bear.

The thirteen years of the lieutenant's
married life were those, therefore, in which
Miss Felicity's adoration was feeblest.

In thirteen years the lieutenant succeeded in breaking his wife's heart, and
ruining his own health. He returned to
his sister a widower with one little girl,
his constitution and his fortunes alike
wrecked, having some time before been
obliged to leave the army, partially para-
lyzed, with a child's helplessness, and a
spoilt child's imperiousness and irritability,
to be a burden for the rest of his life on
the woman he had scarcely noticed while
he had another to worship him. But he
returned; and that to Miss Felicity was
everything. She blotted the tanner's daugh-

ter out of her memory, took the tanner's granddaughter to her heart, accepted her idol again, set it on its old pedestal, with all the strength of her strong will and strong affections, and with a kind of melancholy pleasure in the certainty that if her "Bel bowed down and her Nebo stooped, and were a burden to the weary beast," no one would dispute that burden with her any more.

So she toiled on, and bore her burden, and adored it, her old beautiful god-image, which "cruel circumstances," she said to herself, "and the excess of his own fasci-nations" had shattered, and crowned the old idol with a crown woven out of all the loss and all the possibilities, of all it had been, and of all it might have been.

Year by year she bought the finest cloth for his coats, and day by day she bought the best dainties for his palate, and seated him in the one easy-chair in the sunniest nook of the window in summer, and the warmest corner of the fireside in winter; and when he condescended to that milder degree of grumbling which was his form of thanksgiving, she rejoiced in the character which would have been so lovely but for " the selfish world and the ruthless circumstances which had made him what he was."

It was a provoking ritual to observe from outside, especially to me, not being a worshipper of the lieutenant, and having a reverence little short of worship for the daughter, little Miss Loveday, who was compelled to share in the sacrificial rites.

Of course Miss Felicity had a right to sacrifice herself; but who could have had a right to take all individual hope and pleasure out of that gentle, lovely patient woman's life with all her intellectual and spiritual power, and subordinate her entirely to propping up the ruins of what had never been better than a well-grown animal?

For Miss Loveday was the nearest approach to a saint I knew; and I thank God I had the grace to know it whilst she was amongst us. It is among the saddest of our irrevocable losses when we find out for the first time that some of the holy ones of God have been beside us, for us to consult, learn of, speak to, listen to, only when they have gone from us to be with the goodly company, who are indeed not far from us, but are just beyond speaking distance, out of reach for the time of voice and sight.

My father helped me to the recognition. Miss Loveday had been a friend of my own mother's, and he had the greatest reverence and love for her.

He used to say the poet Cowper must have seen her in spirit when he wrote the lines—

"Artist, attend, your brushes and your paint—
  Produce them ; take a chair, now draw a saint.
Oh, sorrowful and sad ! The streaming tears
Channel her cheeks—a Niobe appears.
Is this a saint ?—throw tints and all away,
True piety is cheerful as the day,—
Will weep, indeed, and heave a pitying groan
For others' woes, but smiles upon her own."

Certainly Loveday Benbow "smiled upon her own" woes with a smile so real and bright, that the woes and saintliness, the burden and the strength which bore it, might easily have been hidden from a careless eye. As to the pitying groan for others' woes, not only could that be relied on for any woes, from the breaking of a child's doll to the breaking of a maiden's heart, but, what is rarer for one whose life is passed in the shadows, she had a smile true and heart-warming as a sunbeam for others' joys, from a child's holiday to a maiden's happiness in being loved, or a mother's joy in loving.

She was a little deaf, and had that sweet inquiring wistfulness in her grey eyes which belongs often to deaf and dumb creatures, human or canine; but so sweet and ready was her sympathy, and so wise her counsel, that she was the natural depository of half the love-confidences in the place; the difficulty and danger of shouting such delicate experiences being nothing to the recompense in the quickness of her comprehension and the fulness of her response.

Clever, or intellectual, were words you would no more have thought of applying to her than to an archangel; and with her heart and brain were so blended, that I have sometimes wondered whether it was that her wit was originally keener than other people's, or that it was sharpened by singleness of purpose; whether it was original force of thought and imagination that made her comprehend every character quickly, or love that quickened thought and imagination into something as unerring as instinct.

My stepmother's insight into character was that of a satirist or of a detective keen to scent out a defect. Miss Felicity's was that of an inspector of the human species, impartial, penetrating, severe but just. Miss Loveday's insight was that of a physician, as keen and as just as either, but deeper, reaching beyond symptoms to causes, to the springs where the disease can be touched and healed.

Sometimes, indeed, she would reproach herself with this quick penetration through disguises and excuses, as if it were not as necessary to the helpers of humanity as to its critics to see truly.

But it is true that the heightening of any one power of nature requires the heightening of every other power to avoid deformity; the growth of every spiritual, as well as every intellectual gift, demands the growth of every other to preserve harmony.

The very truth of Miss Loveday's character which made her perceptions so true would have made her a keener detective than my stepmother, and a severer judge than Miss Felicity, if love had not overwhelmed the bitter in the sweet, and made the justice glow into pity through a deeper faith and a larger hope in God and man.

She always had something of the dove, in my eyes, as Miss Felicity had much of the eagle, and in my darker moments my stepmother not a little of the raven. Doves need sight as keen to defend their brood as eagles to decry their prey. And Miss Loveday's brood were all the human creatures that had need of her. Partly, no doubt, this dove-like grace that encircled her was assisted by her voice, which, as with many deaf people, had a peculiar under-toned softness, like cooings under thick summer leaves; and partly by her dress, which was chiefly replenished from her mother's Quaker wardrobe, in which the prosaic drab was ignored, and the poetical dove-colour and white predominated.

Miss Loveday's dress was what has always seemed to me the loveliest and most becoming of any to middle-aged and elderly women. It retained the Quaker quietness and the delicious Quaker freshness, without the Quaker peculiarities; and her manner was just like her dress. She is fondly enveloped to my memory in a soft grey and white cloud of clothing, which, when I try to analyze it, resolves itself into the whitest of caps, framing her pale sweet face, the neatest of white muslin neckerchiefs folded over her bosom, and the softest of unrustling grey woollen drapery falling in sweeping easy folds around her. Not one sudden, startling, dazzling thing about her in dress, or manner, or voice, not the rustle of silk, or the glitter of a jewel; except the irrepressible occasional twinkle of her kind eyes, and the occasional merry ring which was like an audible twinkle in her soft voice and her laugh.

She was just the opposite (I do not mean the contrary) of Amice Glanvil, who was all mystery and surprise.

The sorrows on which Miss Loveday smiled so radiantly were not sentimental. From her childhood she had been under the yoke unimaginable, unavoidable, of pain ; the yoke which in some respects presses closer on the immortal spirit, and cuts deeper into it than any other, and therefore can in some respects mould it to a more delicate perfection, and furrow it for larger harvests.

No one in Abbot's Weir had been able to fathom the cause.

We had two doctors in Abbot's Weir. One, Dr. Kenton, was of a sanguine temperament, attributed all ailments to debility, and relied for cure chiefly on "nature" and port wine.

The other, Dr. Looseleigh, was of a melancholy disposition, had a strong faith in the depravity of the human constitution, attributed ailments to excess, and hoped for relief, as far as he hoped at all, from bleeding, blistering, and the lowering system in general.

Both medical gentlemen had patients who recovered, and patients who died. But in Abbot's Weir, although theological controversy was mild, the same could not be said of medical. Each generation, whatever its theological proclivities, desires to live as long as it can; debates on what man or system can enable it to live longest, are naturally, therefore not liable to " periods of lukewarmness or declension."

The partisans of Mr. Kenton said that those patients of Mr. Looseleigh who died were killed, actually slain, by his remedies ; and those who recovered, recovered by the force of nature.

The partisans of Mr. Looseleigh said that ·

the patients of Dr. Kenton who recovered struggled through by miracle, or the vigour of an exceptional constitution, and that those who died, perished the victims of neglect, sheer neglect, and faithless contempt of means.

Both systems had been tried on Miss Loveday, but neither successfully. She had been blistered and bled in childhood by Mr. Looseleigh into all but atrophy. She had been "built up" by Dr. Kenton and Miss Felicity into a fever. The only part of either system which she declined was the port wine or brandy. This she resolutely refused. She had promised her mother never to touch either. Dr. Kenton therefore had the advantage in the controversy, in which Miss Loveday's case was a standing weapon. If she could have been induced to break that absurd promise, port wine and nature might have overcome Dr. Looseleigh and disease, and the controversy might have been settled for ever, at least so far as facts can settle controversies. As to those deeper roots in the depths of our own consciousness, whence my father and other sceptical neutrals asserted both systems to arise, those, of course, nothing so superficial as facts and phenomena could have reached.

However, from whatever cause, thus it came to pass that Miss Loveday's yoke was not broken, and she had to suffer and conquer to the end.

Miss Felicity, nevertheless, with whom permanent neutrality was an impossible state of existence, who found it necessary, and therefore practicable, to make up her mind quite decidedly about everything, remained faithful to Dr. Kenton and the port-wine "system," influenced partly, it is believed, by the necessity of seeing some root of good in the evil tendency which had sapped her brother's existence.

It was also believed that the weekly visits

which Dr. Kenton continued to pay had, on
his part at least, a tenderer significance
than Miss Felicity chose to acknowledge.
There had been days when the genial doctor
had paid Miss Felicity the most marked
attentions; and during the years when her
brother's marriage had separated her from
the one ceaseless object of her devotion,
Abbot's Weir had believed that it had detected a gradual softening of the tutelary
Athena manner towards him. It was considered that the prospect of a pleasant home,
a life without care, and an affection which
manifested itself in the flattering form of
respecting her judgment enough to carry on
continual controversies with her, were beginning to melt the impenetrable heart of Miss
Felicity, and that she would soon consent to
be an illustrious case in proof of the suc-
cess of the building-up system.

But her sister-in-law died, the lieutenant
became a helpless invalid, and returned to

receive once more his sister's homage ; and from that moment Dr. Kenton's hopes were blighted.

Miss Felicity returned to her old life-long rôle of priestess and amazon, adoration at her old shrine, and unflinching conflict with infidels and with circumstances for its sake. And Dr. Kenton, after some vain remonstrances, and some years of comparative estrangement, came back, partly by means of his medical care of Miss Loveday, to his old position of admiration and contention; he ceased to sigh, but never ceased to think it worth while to endeavour to put Miss Felicity right on the various points on which they differed ; and to the end the stately brave old gentlewoman had some one who continued to see her with the light of youth on her, and to maintain that she was the finest woman in Abbot's Weir, and had more brains and more spirit than all the men of the town put together.

CHAPTER VIII.

IT was about two years after my father's second marriage that Piers and I were called on to rejoice in the arrival of a step-brother.

Then Mrs. Danescomb's heart awoke. It was as if her whole nature, pent up for forty years, burst forth in that late passion of maternal love.

I believe she tried hard to be just to us all. I believe she tried hard to see what spots there might be in her boy's character. But it was impossible. The rest of the world she continued to see through the same cold, clear, cloudy, frosty, winter daylight in which she had hitherto lived. Around this child glowed and palpitated ceaselessly a flood of tropical sunlight. Faults, of course, her Francis had; her judgment admitted he was human, and her views of humanity in general were unchanged, but with him the deepest shadows glowed with reflected light, like the golden shadows of some rich Venetian picture.

The very nature of the faults he had, moreover, helped to dim her perceptions. He had from childhood no vehement, impetuous outbursts of indignation like those which I was liable to; no earnest entire absorption of his whole being with the subject that interested him, to the forgetfulness of all besides, such as characterized Piers. His character had an external smoothness about it which made the world go smoothly with him. His characteristic motion was gliding: so easy and noiseless was this movement that it was only now and then it struck you that he always contrived to glide into the best place, and into the possession of the

pleasantest things to be attained. We children, of course, who thus lost the pleasantest
things and places early perceived it; but to
our elders it was scarcely ever apparent.
It was always we who created the final dis-
turbance; and what can any government do
when there is a riot but punish the rioters,
deferring the investigation as to who is in
the wrong to a time when the riot and causes
have ceased to be of moment.

Francis was found in tranquil possession
of the coveted delights, toy or picture book,
or place in the game; possession is nine points
of the law; tranquillity the desideratum of
all governments in the world; why could we
not have left our little brother alone?

Thus we who were continually being
robbed and wronged were the perpetual
plaintiffs; and the world has no mercy on
perpetual plaintiffs. Francis, "poor little
darling," as his mother truly said, "was
never heard to raise his sweet little voice."

whilst I, at least, was in one continual wail and clamour.

Even our father often gave the verdict against us. "The world was large," he would say, "and Francis was little; why did we just want the thing the poor little fellow had set his heart on, and was so peaceably enjoying?"

In vain we pleaded rights which we knew to be unquestionable; what can be more tiresome, or seem more selfish, than to be always pleading one's rights, especially against what is apparently the weaker party?

"Why were we always shrieking about our rights? Brothers and sisters should not think about rights. They should be always ready to "give up" to each other, and to do as they should be done by?

So, between my stepmother's fondness, my father's generosity, and interpretations of the Sermon on the Mount which drove me wild with the impossibility of combating them, and the certainty of their being wrong, the tyranny of our little brother was established.

This was a state of things, however, that could not long continue unbroken.

At length my stepmother once more proposed that Piers and I should be sent to Miss Felicity's school.

My father had long opposed this, having certain theories of education, partly derived from Rousseau's Emile, not at all in harmony with Miss Felicity's.

He wished that education should be restored to what he considered its true meaning, of leading out the faculties; should be not so much a putting in as calling out, should be a development of growth from within, not the fitting on of an iron frame to contract and cramp growth from without. Theories which are now worn threadbare and colourless with discussion or use were then fresh and full of bloom. And all such ideas Miss

Felicity considered altogether chimerical and Utopian.

"Calling out faculties," said she. "The only faculty she knew that could always be sure of coming at the call, was the faculty of mischief. No putting in? What then was the good of learning to read at all? She supposed Piers and I would not develop out of ourselves even the multiplication table, unless it was put into us, still less the history of the Greeks and Romans, or the gods and heroes. Not that she saw much use in history," she would somewhat cynically admit. "What was there in it but wise men's words and foolish men's deeds? Things which, if they had happened in a neighbour's house instead of in palaces, you would have taken care the children did not hear. But the Greeks and Romans, and the gods and heroes, and the multiplication table, as the world was, had to be learned, and Mr. Danescombe might wait some time for a new world, or for a generation of children who came into it with their little minds filled already."

My poor father had certainly seen considerable faculty for not getting on developed in Piers and me since our little brother's arrival, and accordingly at last he waived his theory, and abandoned us to Miss Felicity and the "rote system." To us the school meant simply Miss Felicity, and a very awful personality we considered her. My father was in the second stage of human progress, the age of philosophical system and theory; whilst Miss Felicity had advanced to the third, contemptuously ignoring systems and philosophies, and recognising nothing but facts and phenomena; and Piers and I remained in the earliest, seeing nothing but persons and personifications.

From the beginning, I think, although most kindly disposed towards us, Miss Felicity nevertheless regarded us as rather dangerous little persons, brought up in no

one knows what heretical persuasions con-
cerning the rights and the wrongs of man.

The years of our school-life were among
the most reactionary years England ever saw.

Not an abuse but was rooted in its place,
and not a harvest of reform but was stunted
and nipped by the French Reign of Terror.

Old Tories like Miss Felicity glorified
their narrowest political prejudices into
articles of the Creed, when the Revolution
and his own heroic patience had consecrated
the French king into a martyr. Benevolent
and tranquil men of progress like my father
had to defend themselves as if they had
been Jacobins. Mild Whigs like Dr.
Kenton, who looked for the general im-
provement of the world on the same sanguine and genial principles on which he
looked for the general recovery of his
patients, simply turned a little round the
other way, and became for the moment mild
Tories.

"What do you say now, Dr. Kenton,"
Miss Felicity would triumphantly demand,
"to your Reformers and Jacobins?"

"I say, Miss Felicity," he would reply,
"what I always said. Above all things no
convulsions, no violence to the constitution.
If nature cannot throw off the ailment for
herself, we must assist her a little, Miss
Felicity, gently assist her. That is what I
mean by reform. If our assistance fails, we
must let her alone and wait, Miss Felicity,
tranquilly wait."

Mild Tories, on the other hand, like my
uncle Fyford and Mr. Rabbidge, those who
were Conservative from fear, became rabid
Tories, also from fear. They would have
established a Reign of Terror of their own
on behalf of our glorious constitution,
would "keep the mob down, sir," said my
uncle to my father, "by fire and sword, if
necessary by the gibbet, or the—"

"*The stake*," suggested my father drily.

My uncle scarcely heeded the interruption. "Are we to have our houses burnt about our ears," he said, "by a set of fanatics calling themselves philanthropists and reformers?"

And it was through this tempest of prejudice and reaction that the noble band of religious men who had set their hearts on abolishing the great wrong of the African slave-trade, steadfastly went on with the conflict, and ten times brought in the measure ten times defeated in a House of Commons, excited to a fury of reaction, elected by a nation goaded to a contempt of all progress by the fury and madness of the three years' terrible reaction against centuries of oppression in France.

It was, no doubt, this state of things, of course at the time unknown to us, which brought me into the two difficulties which now recur to my mind.

One sunny Sunday afternoon Piers and I were sitting on the step of our arbour on the highest terrace of the garden. He was playing with Pluto and I was reading intently with my elbows on my knees, so intently, that I did not see my father and my stepmother with little Francis, my uncle Fyford, and Dick approaching up the steep slope, until they were close at hand.

I was especially absorbed with the book, because I ignorantly thought it was about to throw some light on the "Duty to our Neighbour," and the Sermon on the Mount, especially as connected with my stepmother and Francis, which might bring the Christian code within reach of my practice. There were passages in it about "natural rights," about the "great sin being making each other unhappy," which I thought excellent; also a passage asserting that "the Duty of Man is not a wilderness of turnpike-gates between us and our Maker, through which we pass by ticket from one to the other, but plain and simple, consisting in our duty to God as His by *birth* and *family*, and in doing what we would be done by," which I thought clearer than the Catechism, at least with my stepmother's commentary.

My uncle startled me by an approving pat on the head.

"Well done, little maid! Quite a little Lady Jane Grey! Is it Plato, or 'The Whole Duty of Man?'"

"It is not so much about our *duties* as about our *rights*," I said. "I found it in the Summer Parlour." And I gave the volume confidingly into his hands.

He started as if he had been stung, dashed it from him to the ground, and ground his heel into it as if it had been a viper.

"Piers Danescombe, I could not have expected this even of toleration like yours:

Tom Paine's 'Rights of Man'—such poison in the hands of this poor innocent babe!"

"Indeed, Uncle Fyford," I said, thinking that I had in some way compromised my father, "it is a Sunday book. It is not a story book. The gentleman who wrote it seems to dislike the Bastille and slavery as much as father, and war as much as Miss Loveday. And he speaks about our Father in heaven, Uncle Fyford. Indeed it is a Sunday book."

"Listen to the poor innocent!" said Uncle Fyford. "It is enough to pierce one's heart."

"Bride, my darling," said my father, in his dry quiet way, "Tom Paine's 'Rights of Man' is not exactly the book for you. If I had had any idea that your tastes lay in that direction, I would have labelled it, 'Not good for little girls.' But, Richard," he continued, turning to my uncle, "if wise men would take the good in that book and use it, they would do more to neutralise the harm in it than by railing at it in a mass for ever."

" Good in Tom Paine !" said my uncle, roused beyond his usual decorum. " I am sick of your *'good in everything.'* I believe you would find good in the devil."

" *There might have been !* you know," said my father, very gravely. His simple quiet words startled me like a flash of lightning. They made me feel that he felt the existence of the devil to be a very real and sorrowful fact, instead of the half ridiculous, half terrible, mythical legend handed down to us in the nursery.

Mrs. Danescombe intervened.

"That is precisely what I am always saying to Mr. Danescombe, Dr. Fyford," she said. " Good in everything there may be, though I confess I have not found it, and I believe it is not the Bible, but only Shakspere that asserts it. But evil in everything most certainly there is, at least in every person. And I can never see we remove it by blinding our eyes to it."

"Well, Euphrasia," said my father, "you look for the evil and I for the good; so, between us, I hope we shall strike the balance. Only, if we both reach the better world, you will be so unfortunate as to have lost your occupation, while mine can continue for ever."

"Wait till you are there, Piers," rejoined my uncle. "At all events, you won't find Tom Paine's 'Rights of Man' there."

"No," replied my father, "the book will have done its work, good and evil, here below."

"Evil enough!" said my uncle; "good, only as Satan did good to Job, by landing him, with his potsherd, among the ashes."

My investigations into the "natural rights" of man were, however, checked: a check the less painful to me because even Mr. Paine did not give me any light on the natural "rights of women" or of little girls. I was sent back to the Ten Commandments and to the Duty to my Neighbours.

The only result that remained from my inopportune pursuit of knowledge was the rare felicity of a little direct religious lesson from my father.

That evening he took me on his knee in the Oak Parlour. Piers had gone to bed, and my stepmother was putting Francis to sleep, so that we were alone. And above us was that picture of my mother, present to the consciousness of us both."

"Bride, my darling," he said, "Duties are better things for us to think about than Rights."

"If other people would only think about our rights a little, father," I ventured to murmur, "then it would be very nice to have nothing to think about but our duties. But they don't. They only think about their own rights, and our duties."

"Very true, Bride," he said. "They don't, and they won't. And that is the way there is so much troublesome history for you and me to learn. But you know some one must begin. Suppose you and I begin at the other end. *Our own duties, and other people's rights.* You will find much more good come of it in the end."

Then, the only time I can remember, he led me to my mother's picture and stood before it with his hand on my shoulder.

"That was what she did, my child. God gave her one of his lambs to keep, and she kept it well as long as she was here. God help me to keep it for Him and for her better than I have."

"Oh, father, you can't keep us better," I said.

That lesson was brief, but it accomplished

its end. It brought me back to my duties, instead of to his and to my stepmother's.

It was not very long after this that Piers and I fell into another difficulty, at Miss Felicity's school.

I remember this with especial distinctness, because it was the beginning of Piers and my entering into closer relations with Amice Glanvil and our sweet bright Claire Angélique des Ormes.

A week before, the three spare rooms in Miss Felicity's house had been engaged and occupied by three foreigners, refugees from France, Madame la Marquise des Ormes, her little daughter Claire Angélique, and Léontine, a vivacious maid, who governed and protected them both, and would fain have governed Miss Felicity, and all Abbot's Weir, had this been possible to any Frenchwoman.

Madame had only been seen, a slight fragile lady, leaning rather feebly on the arm of Léontine, and greeting Miss Felicity as she entered the arched door with such a courtly reverence as Abbot's Weir had not previously dreamed of.

Léontine had been seen and heard abundantly, making her presence felt like a wind through house and town.   Little Claire had only been heard prattling in a sweet voice to her mother in the parlour inside the schoolroom until that momentous afternoon when she appeared under Miss Felicity's wing, but not under her rod, as a kind of amateur scholar.

It was an August afternoon, very sultry. The room was long and low : Miss Felicity was fettered by no goverment regulations as to cubic feet of air and space. Of space there was enough; of air certainly not enough to keep forty children awake. Miss Felicity would on no account have exposed her lessons to the intrusion of the street by opening the window.

Want of ozone, therefore, was telling powerfully on the intellects of the pupils, and on the temper of the mistress. The flies were drowsily buzzing now and then against the panes, the black cat sleepily purring on the window-seat, too lazy even to wink at my stepmother's cat on the opposite window. Many of the children out of reach of the rod had yielded to sleep, and the rest were hopelessly struggling against it, when the question came in a sharp voice from Miss Felicity—

"Bridget Danescombe, who were the heroes?"

I must have been half asleep myself, for I remember instantly sitting up trying to look especially wide awake, as is the wont with persons so surprised, and responding desperately to the last word which I had caught.

"Father says there are some in France, Miss Felicity. He said so last night. They pulled down a wicked place called the Bastille."

Miss Felicity's colour rose. I think she did not know whether I said it in simplicity or in malice.

"Bridget Danescombe," she repeated, slightly rapping my fingers to recall my attention, "think what you are saying. Who were the *heroes ?*"

"And some, father said, there are in England," I continued, divided between anxiety to sustain myself by that infallible judgment, and dread of the well-known little ebony ruler. "They want to pull down the slave-trade and the impressment —he said impressment. These are our Bastilles. I know he said they were heroes. And the only name I remember is Granville Sharp."

"Silly child, dreaming as usual," said Miss Felicity, diplomatically passing by the perilous answer, and admonishing me

by a severe rap on my knuckles. "I pass
to your brother—two years your younger
and ten years your better. Piers Danescombe, who were the heroes?"

Whatever could have been thought of
the spirit of my answer, there could have
been no doubt as to that which rang
through the tones of Piers. His was a
response, not to Miss Felicity's question,
but to her rap on my fingers.

"Sister Bride is right, Miss Felicity,"
he said. "Father did say so, only last
night."

By this time the little community was
thoroughly aroused, with true British instinct scenting the battle from afar.

"Yes, indeed, Miss Felicity," I ventured,
"father said impressing seamen and trading
in slaves was as bad as shutting people up
in the Bastille; and Mr. Granville Sharp
was a hero for trying to stop it. I remember quite well that was the hero's name,

and also that he wants to stop people having slaves, because that is wicked."

I had rushed on impetuously, forgetful of all but the purpose in hand, when, looking up, I saw Amice Glanvil's great mysterious eyes fixed fully on me, not in anger, but with a look of grave wonder and questioning.

She looked a shade more pallid than usual, but I flushed crimson. I remembered the black nurse and the negro footmen, and I felt so sorry I should have said anything to grieve my princess.

But I had not much time for reflection. For then out and spoke Dick Fyford.

"Miss Felicity, if Bride Danescombe were not a girl, so that no one can do anything to her, she would not dare. My own uncle is a sea captain, and I am going to sea, and he says people who cry out against impressment are traitors and fools. I heard him. The king's navy could not be kept up without, and then the French would come

and kill the king and burn up London, and
Abbot's Weir, and all of us."

The conflict was becoming perilous. Was
Miss Felicity's class of mythology—extra
—to prepare the more aristocratic classes
for Mr. Rabbidge, and to distinguish them
from the common herd, to end in this?

Had not Mrs. Rabbidge, always a little
too eagerly alive to the growth of Miss
Felicity's pupils into her husband's, de-
nounced the mythology as a poaching on
his demesnes? And had not Mr. Rabbidge himself mildly admitted that Miss
Felicity was meddling with matters too
high for her?

And was it to be said that such frightful
Jacobinism had been uttered in her presence
unavenged?

The case was perplexing. On the score
of politics it could not be taken up. Piers
and I had appealed to Cæsar in the person
of our father, and to Miss Felicity paternal

authority was a foundation of all other authority, by no means to be lightly interfered with.

She therefore recurred to history, and wisely chose to treat me as a dunce rather than as a heretic.

" Bridget Danescombe knows better," she asserted. " The heroes lived in Greece. They come after the heathen gods. There were Hercules and Perseus,—and others," said Miss Felicity, not having a book, and judiciously becoming vague. " They fought with dragons. And the heroes and the dragons have all been dead and gone thousands of years. Bridget Danescombe, I am sorry; but I must put the fool's-cap on you, and you must sit on that stool in the middle of the school. Take this book and learn the names of the heroes. When you have learned them you may come down."

And so saying she took off my little

mob-cap, put on the terrible cone of brown paper, and made me climb on the tall stool. Thus were the germs of Jacobinism crushed; and thus was I set up as a beacon to juvenile Abbot's Weir. Piers came and stood beside me, his eyes flashing and his face crimson, in defiance of authority. Wisely Miss Felicity took no notice. Her government was too strong for her to delight in petty irritating revenges.

I was too proud to cry, and too bewildered by anger and shame to learn. And yet by some strange instinct of justice, I made a distinction between my stepmother and Miss Felicity.

My stepmother had never rapped my knuckles or set me on a stool, or punished me in any way. And yet her cold "Bridget!" hurt me more than Miss Felicity's ruler, or even her fool's-cap, terrible as that was.

I felt that Miss Felicity in some unac-

countable way had misunderstood my
words. I did not feel that she misunderstood and misjudged *me*. And after a little
while, getting used to my position, I found
myself endeavouring to account, not for
my conduct (in this instance I had the
great and unusual happiness of a clear conscience), but for Miss Felicity's, and to
justify her.

This, of course, did not help me to learn
my "heroes," but it quieted my mind, and
the book served as a veil as I held it before
my face.

And so the minutes passed on, until the
bell rang for the school to close.

We always finished in the morning with
the grace before meals, and in the evening
with a verse of the evening prayer.

For this purpose Miss Felicity told me to
come down from my elevation.

To this instant my heart beats faster as I
think how that sweet little French girl

Claire, not of course being in the awe of our punishments and rules of ordinary scholars, glided forward to me before any one could stop her, with her easy French grace, and helped me down, and kissed my cheek, her first kiss, *with the fool's-cap still on*, and led me to Miss Felicity, and asked her in sweet broken English to take the cap off, which Miss Felicity very kindly and rather nervously did. And then Claire herself, with her lissom fingers, arranged my hair under my little cap, and kissed my quivering lips, for I was bursting into tears. Then, apparently summoned from the room within, she waved her hand to all of us and curtseyed like a fairy queen, and disappeared within the door of her mother's apartment.

Piers and I, of course, were kept in that day, until I had 'learned the mythology. And meantime Miss Felicity went out and left us alone, with Amice Glanvil, who was kneeling on the window-seat, waiting for the negro nurse.

When Miss Felicity was gone, Amice came down noiselessly from the window-seat, and suddenly stood before me.

I looked up from the book, and met those dark wistful eyes for the first time, not turned away from me, but gazing steadily into mine, through my eyes, I felt, into me.

"Who said it was *wicked to have slaves?*" she asked.

My eyes sank before her gaze.

"It was my father," I said in a low voice. I wished to say something in excuse, but I could find nothing.

"But people need *not* be wicked who have slaves," she said. "My father was good, and he had slaves. And he is dead. He was not wicked. And I was born with slaves. How can we help what we are born with?"

She spoke very low, with a deep voice

and a clear lingering utterance, which to me sounded foreign. The question was beyond me.

" You can be kind to them," I said feebly. That was all I could think of.

" Some old Greek people set them free," said Piers thoughtfully, more childlike than I; that is what my father said Mr. Granville Sharp wanted. You can *set them free*," he said, with a boy's directness, "that is the only way, I think, of being kind to slaves."

Amice Glanvil turned her penetrating glance on him, as if to look him through; but his frank, blue eyes met hers, with a steady gaze, and bore the scrutiny.

" *Set them free!* Piers Danescombe," she said. " You do not know in the least what you are talking about. But you have given me the answer at the very bottom of your thoughts, and I thank you." For she was not in the least like a child, our princess.

The negro nurse came to fetch her, and interrupted our conversation.

But when she was wrapped up in her gold and crimson splendours she turned back to us, and took one of our hands in each of hers.

" Bride Danescombe," she said, " I like you, I have known and liked you a long time, and I like you better to-day. Piers Danescombe, you are a little boy, and do not know in the least what you said. But you speak the truth, and hardly any one does. And I like you too. I will ask Granny. And you will come and see me. Good-bye."

I felt honoured as by a royal invitation ; but Piers was cooler, and said, " We will see."

I got up on the window-seat and looked after Miss Amice in a flutter of delight. I forgot all about the heroes. I felt sure I had found my heroine. The spell of silent years was broken; our princess had spoken to us, and the enchanted palace would be sure to open.

Then a soft voice called me from the corner where little Miss Loveday had been lying on her couch, correcting exercises unobserved by any of us.

"Dear child," she said, "dear little Bride, let me help thee. Aunt Felicity will come back, and thee will have learned nothing."

In a few minutes she had taught me the lesson.

And when Miss Felicity returned I said it to her perfectly.

I think she was anxious to make some amends to me. I had suffered as a victim to great public considerations, as I did not know, but she did. But I felt there was no personal wrong intended, and I felt no resentment against her. And when she took my hand kindly, and said I had a good father and mother, and she hoped I would be a good little girl, I took courage, and looking up in her face said, "Miss Felicity, father said *you* were one of the heroes, too."

"Nonsense! nonsense, child!" she said, colouring. But I saw that the keen eyes moistened, and she took me to Miss Love-day and said, in a tremulous voice—

"Loveday, the child grows more like her poor dear mother every day—I saw it on that stool to-day—and she has just that sweet forgiving temper. And, please God, the poor little maid shall never stand there again. It was a mistake of mine, and it cut me to the heart. There," she added, laughing, "there's a foolish thing for a mistress to say to a child. Foolish old woman and foolish little Bride. How shall I keep you in order now? You will never be afraid of the ruler and the fool's-cap more."

But I began to *love* Miss Felicity. And

oh the good it did me to hear a grown-up woman actually confess she had made a mistake and done wrong !

It restored to me my ideal of justice. It made me feel there was *one* right way for little children and grown people.

From that day I would not have offended or grieved Miss Felicity for the world.

But when she left the room Miss Loveday put her arm around me and said—

" Little Bride, it is quite right to learn about the old heroes. All little boys and girls must. But never thou give up believing in the heroes and saints *now*. That is the great matter for us. Never give up looking for them, little Bride, and always expecting to see them. It is a pity not to know the heroes of long ago. But the most terrible mistake we can make, any of us, is not to learn to know the heroes and saints God is making to-day, who are with us now, because that is like misunderstanding

God Himself, and our dear Lord and Saviour, and the blessed, loving Spirit, and putting Him far back into history, among the Greeks and Romans.

"Never think the saints and heroes are all dead and gone, Piers and Bride. It is like thinking our Lord is dead, and his living Spirit with us no more. That is the mistake people who went wrong made in every age. Look for them, expect to find them in the world—in your little world—now, and look to God, who is always making them, and you will find them. And then stick close to them, my dears, and follow them, whatever they are called and whatever they look like ; and, in that way, you may grow like them too. Oh, thank God, Bride," she added in a low voice, "I did ask God long ago for this ; and He heard me, and showed me your mother. He showed her to me before she went away. And that has helped me all my life. Never, never think the saints and heroes are living no longer upon earth. The heroes are not dead, nor the dragons; nor are the saints gone to heaven, or their crosses. Look up and keep your heart open, and you will find them, my poor little ones, never fear."

I tried to say something to her, but I could not. My voice would not come.

For when father had said Miss Felicity was a hero, he had also said that Miss Loveday was a saint.

But I smiled all through my heart as I went across to the market-place, to think how much sooner than Miss Loveday had expected her words had begun to come true.

CHAPTER IX.

THERE are many mornings in our lives, many moments which are as fountains, from which the rest of our life continues to flow.

The old promise has been kept. Day and night, winter and summer, seed-time and harvest, have not failed.

And hereafter, also (I trust), it will be thus. It is in a pagan Elysium, not in a Christian Paradise, that "everlasting spring" abides.

What are blossoms which never ripen into fruit but painted shows? What is childhood which never awakens into manhood but a dwarfed or undeveloped humanity? What are seed-times which have

no harvest but promises perpetually renewed
and never fulfilled ?

"*No night there*" must mean no darkness, no bewilderment, no losing our way,
no missing our end, no horror of doubt, no
shadow of death; certainly not, no fresh
mornings. So often we confuse divine
suggestions by vulgarising symbols into
pictures, or by hammering out poetical
images into prosaic parables !

Again and again in our lives "God takes
us by the hand," as the old Moravian hymn
sings, "and says, Start afresh."

Here, indeed, our fresh startings are made
necessary, too often, by our wanderings
from the way, or our weariness of the way.
But the fulness of life there will surely not
be less rich in variety and glorious growth
than the hindered and fluctuating and fail-
ing life here. For ever it will be walking
in "newness of life." O wondrous fulness of joy, when all the past shall

enrich, not burden and sadden, the present;
when before the heart, satisfied with the
present in His presence, shall spread endless ranges of hope in the future, also in
His presence!

We shall not be gods hereafter, but
children of God; and, for ever, in our
Father's hand, will be infinite possibilities
of growth unforeseen by us, and divine sur-
prises of bliss.

One such morning, or fountain head, in
my life was that memorable afternoon when
Miss Felicity exalted me to the stool of
repentance and crowned me with the fool's-
cap, and afterwards exalted herself and
human nature in my sight by confessing
herself in the wrong, and crowned me with
the kiss of reconciliation, which scaled me
her loyal subject thereafter.

For then and there three great friendships
of my life began: that dear discipleship to

Loveday Benbow—that tender affection to Claire des Ormes, half motherly, half lover-like — that faithful " cameraderie " with Amice Glanvil in many a pull " against the stream."

Before that day, in looking back, it seems as if life had still been cradled in the mountain tarn, mirroring the little world around, filling its own little cup. After that it began to flow.

And not mine, but my brother's also, which was in many ways more than my own to me. Our lives began to flow ; and they began to part, into those two streams of womanhood and manhood which are each one so much more for being two,—so much more to each other, so much more to the world.

In the first place, it was just after that morning that for the first time I remember Piers took an opposite course to me.

When, in due time, the invitation came

for us from Madam Glanvil to spend a holiday with Amice at Court, he would not go.

He was not quite ten, and I was not quite thirteen. I had in my small way been "a mother to him" for so many years! His refusal surprised me greatly.

My father did not seem displeased at Piers declining; indeed, he appeared to wonder a little at my delight in accepting.

Mrs. Danescombe, on the contrary, commended me. She said it was a very desirable house to visit at, and she was pleased to see me appreciate it.

"It is a big house, certainly, Bride," said my father; "but you know we do not grow bigger by being in big houses."

"Mr. Danescombe," remonstrated my stepmother, "let me entreat you not to teach Jacobinism to Bride: for girls at least it cannot be suitable."

"It is not the house, father," I said; "it is Amice."

"Amice, with the glory of the big house about her," he said, "and the black servants, and the sedan-chair. How long have you known Miss Glanvil?"

"Oh, father," I said, "all our lives long."

"A very extensive period," he said. "I did not know you had ever spoken to each other."

"No, not exactly *spoken* until yesterday," I said, "but *looked*, and understood each other always."

He laughed, and said no more.

But in the evening I endeavoured to shake Piers's resolution.

We were sitting in that very miscellaneous lumber-room, music-room, and workshop of my father's, called the Summer Parlour.

I was planning Armadas, and talking of great naval campaigns. (We were just at the outbreak of the first war with the

French Republic.) Piers was constructing a little ship; a division of labour frequent between us. He was essentially a maker, not a critic, except as far as criticism is necessary to construction. Whilst I was content with anything that would float, his quick eye caught the angles and curves which made the difference between swift and slow sailing. He was never satisfied until the little vessel was as perfect as his accurate hands could make it. I believe from early years he had an opinion that the talking of the world is mostly to be done by women, and by men who cannot, or will not, work.

"You will not go to Court, Piers?" I said. "It never can be because Amice called you a ' little boy ? ' "

He laughed.

" How like a girl, sister ! " he said (not satirically; I never heard him say a satirical thing in his life, his nature was too down-

right and too sweet. Later in life I know
he thought satire only the poor refuge of
people who could not fight the battles), "not
like *you !* What difference can calling me
anything make? Besides, I *am* a little boy,
rather; and I like Amice Glanvil. She is
almost as good as a boy herself."

Feminine and masculine distinctions were
becoming very pronounced. My Protec-
torate was evidently tottering; and also
I felt a little jealous.

" I don't believe boys like girls better for
being like boys," I said; "at least, only
quite little boys do. Claire des Ormes is not
like a boy; and I am sure you like her."

" She is not like a boy or a girl, or anything," he replied.

" Less?" I said.

" No, you know very well, sister," he
said, "*more !*"

" Yes, I think so," I said. " When she
kissed me, it felt as if it had been the queen.

What *is* she like? A fairy? or a princess? or an angel? or a hero?"

"How can we tell, sister? We never saw either. Only it would be worth while to do something for her, like what she did for you."

"Yes," I said, "it would. But there is nothing to do."

"Something always comes to do," he said, "when we are ready."

It was a cheerful view of life, and more axiomatic than Piers knew.

We had wandered from Amice and Court.

"And you will not go to Court? Not if father wishes it?"

"Father does not care," he said.

Which I knew was true.

"Not to see Amice? who is nearly as good as a boy, and all those wonderful monkeys, and parrots, and models, and museums?"

"I can see Amice at school," he said.

"Oh Piers, why won't you? Not with *me*?"

"Sister Bride, I *cannot*," he said. "I cannot be waited on by slaves."

We had heard so many stories of the wrongs and cruel hardships of slavery!

I had cried over them so many times; and planned so many wonderful schemes of rescue; and had sometimes thought Piers rather lukewarm on the subject.

And meantime, the griefs which had melted into tearful dewdrops with me, had been entering into his very heart.

I could say no more.

So, I went alone to Court.

It was more awful than I expected. I was met at the door by the two black footmen, and ushered with bows through the hall, museum, and dining-room, into the large withdrawing-room.

No one was there; and alone in those

great stately rooms, among the ancestral
portraits and the ancestral chairs, and the
Japanese cabinets; alone, without Piers to
matronise, I felt a very little girl indeed.
And that uncomfortable consciousness of
clothes not quite duly identified with me,
which through my stepmother's monitions
had become the spectre of my darker
moments, came on me.

Only until Amice came in, and by her
presence filled the grand old rooms with life,
not rushing or gushing, by any means, but
with that essential reality and absence of
self-consciousness about her which always
made everything of the nature of clothes
and conventionalities sink into due sub-
ordination.

That, I suppose, was partly what Piers
meant by her being like a boy.

She came forward and took my hand.

"Where is Piers?" she said, "your
little brother?"

My eyes fell.

"He could not—did not—come," I said, in some confusion.

"*Would* not," she said decidedly. "He is a strange little boy, but I like him."

She seemed to me rather candid about my kindred.

"He is the dearest brother in the world," I said.

"No doubt," she said, "to you. He is your own. You are not in the least alike. But I like *you*."

She never asked if we liked her.

"You have another brother who is not like either of you," she said; "very little. I do not like him. He looks as if he had been born old."

That was unfortunate; for my stepmother, I knew, looked on my friendship at Court as an introduction for Francis.

I began to think her confidences as to the family had better stop.

But she continued.

"I like your father; he is a gentleman, although he does think it wicked to have slaves. I am glad your mother is only your stepmother. She is like your little brother. And I always want her to be well tossed about in a wind. A storm at sea would be best. That shakes one out of many things."

It was very curious to find we had all been looked at and through so long, by those wistful, inquiring eyes.

And here was a new and most interesting glimpse into her former life!

"You have been in a storm at sea! That must be wonderful," I said, not sorry to reverse the telescope and turn it on her own life.

"Yes. I liked it," she said; "especially when it was dangerous."

She had her hat in her hand; she put it on and led me into the garden.

"The waves were very high?" I asked.

"It was not the waves I liked," she replied, "it was the people. It was as good as the play, indeed it was much better, because it was the other way. Every one changed characters—changed into themselves. It was great fun. People who had told wonderful stories of their killing lions and tigers, and frightening slaves, turned quite white, and wrung their hands, and kept questioning the captain, like women, if there was any danger? And one man, who had laughed at the Methodists, and had sworn big oaths, actually came and asked my poor Chloe to pray for him. It was capital fun."

I began to think her rather elfish and hard-hearted—"cynical" I should have said had I known the word.

"Chloe is a Methodist," I replied, rather evasively. "I know a Methodist too, old Reuben Pengelly."

"Yes," she said; "the old man with the

violoncello, in a scarlet waistcoat. Chloe
loves him like a brother. And Chloe heard
from him about you. He loves you all so
much. Only Granny won't let her go often
to the meetings. She says it gives those
poor creatures notions."

"What notions?" I said, rising out of
my life-long awe of Amice, with some indignation. "No one would get anything but
good notions from Reuben."

"Good notions for white people, very
likely," she replied; "but white people
and black are not the same. At least, so
Granny says. I am not sure; however, it
makes very little difference to Chloe. For
she has her notions, wherever she is, and
they make her very happy."

"What notions make her happy?" I
asked.

"That God is very good, and loves every
one, black and white. That He can make
black people have white hearts," she replied

softly. " It makes her very happy. But I cannot quite see it. At least, if I were black I should find it difficult to think God had cared much, or taken much trouble about me."

" I did not see it once," I said, "till Reuben showed me."

" Did not see *what?* " she said, looking full into my eyes.

" That God was good to *me*," I said.

"To *you!*" she replied, rather scornfully. " Then you must certainly have been very cross and ungrateful. *I* can see that plainly enough. You have a father and a brother ! "

" He had taken away *Mother !* " I said. It nearly choked me to say it, but I felt I must. " And I *was* ungrateful, and did not understand Him. But I do now ! "

She smiled a little peculiar smile of her own, sarcastic but not severe.

" *Understand God !* " she said, with a

strange depth in her tone. "That is a good deal for a little girl. You are a year younger than I am. Reuben told Chloe."

"Understand that He is my Father, and is good, always," I said, "to every one."

"That is a good deal too!" she said in a low tone, "more than I do. But Chloe does. She says our Saviour let a black man carry his cross. I am not quite sure of that. Because, they were not all black then in Africa, the history says. That is the worst of history. It disturbs so many nice notions. But Chloe knows nothing of history, at least only that one History. And it comforts her to think of that black man carrying the cross. Why I can't exactly see, even if it is true."

"Ah, Amice, I can see!" I said. "Wouldn't you have liked to carry it for Him?"

She paused a moment, and then said, very slowly and gravely—

" If He had given it to me. But He did
not. It was only the Romans."

" It is almost always the Romans or the
Jews who do lay things like that on people,"
I said. "But it was *his* cross. Ah, I do
think I should have liked that ! To have
helped Him a little ! "

" I think you would," she said, with a
sort of tenderness that had not been in her
voice before. " *I* would rather have beaten
off the Jews and the soldiers."

" I should not like to have been the
Romans ! " she added, very low and sadly.
" Do you think any one *can* be like that
now ? " she asked, with one of her sudden,
inquiring looks, as if she would surprise an
answer out of one's eyes.

The whole meaning flashed on me, and I
was dumb.

" Because," she said, " if *that* History is
always going on, as Chloe seems to think,
there must always be the two sides, and

one would like to be sure on which side one is."

"Do you care for flowers?" she resumed, changing her tone and subject suddenly. "I don't; unless they are wild. Furze and heather on the down, when one is galloping over it, are nice. But in beds they are tiresome. And especially in green-houses—mere *things* in pots. It is dreadful to have to grow up. When I am seventeen I shall have to show Granny's visitors round the green-houses, and listen to them saying how gorgeous this flower is, and how lovely that leaf is, on and on for ever. Animals are what I like. They are so queer, and yet so fond of one. And one can so easily make them happy. And they have no souls, which is a great comfort, when creatures belong to one; it saves one from so much perplexity. At least, no souls that can be lost; no conscience; that is the

troublesome thing. Are you sure they have
no souls of some kind? Dogs now, and
some horses look as if they had some kind
of souls *growing* in them, something *beginning* to be a soul. Don't you think so?"

I had never speculated on the psychology
of animals. My chief personal attach-
ments had been among cats, except indeed
Pluto.

"I certainly never thought my stepmother's cat had a soul," I said. "If it
has, it must be such a very bad one, I am
sure I hope it hasn't. And I am sure it
has no conscience. Nor my own kittens.
They purr and rub against one, and are so
soft and comfortable that I never thought of
their wanting anything more."

"Cats? Certainly not!" she replied,
decidedly. "I always think, one could have
made a cat oneself, almost. All fur and
purr, and wanting to be stroked. That is,
some cats. There are others, like tigers, all

cunning and stealth, and spite, one could *not* have made, *would* not if one could. Ah, Bride! (may I call you Bride? It is so much more like you than Bridget) how many puzzles there are! Does it not seem as if the devil must have created some things?"

"The devil *create* anything!" I said indignantly. "No! God—the good God-created everything, and created everything good."

"It is not all very good just now," she said, shaking her head. "At all events, the devil has spoiled a great deal."

All this was said at intervals, as she was showing me round the place, garden, rabbit-hutches, pheasantry, poultry-yard, her own horse in the stables, where the great blood-hound fawned on her, and the large stag-hound put his paws on her shoulders in a rapture of welcome.

"There!" she said, "down, Leo! poor

fellow! Dogs one certainly could never have made."

"Some creatures love me, Bride, you see," she added. "I am not sure that *you* do. You think me too like a boy. You see I was the only child, there was no son, only a daughter, and I have to do for both."

She did care, then, to be loved. So daring and apparently independent, yet so sensitive to every change of feeling in those she cared about—she, too, had need of love, as much as I had.

For I had been feeling just a little doubtful about her; and she knew it as well as if I had said all I felt, in plainer words than I could have found.

We came to the kitchen garden.

"I like this," she said. "The vegetables have something to do. They are not like the flowers, fine ladies living to be looked at. Especially geraniums and dahlias, and

camellias. They are as if they were stiffen-
ing into wax-work. Some of the flowers are
just sweet and lovely because they cannot
help it; and so natural and full of life, no
gardeners can spoil them. Roses, lilies of
the valley, the great white queen lily, and
violets. But vegetables, poor things, are
always doing their best in an honest and
simple way, and not thinking about themselves. And the flowers in kitchen gardens
are always the nicest, don't you think? I
suppose the company of the useful humble
creatures improves them."

Then she led me silently to a mouldy little
arbour in an angle of the wall.

"Don't you hate arbours?" she said.
"They are the most ridiculous things.
They are neither open air nor indoors.
And I hate all things and people that are
neither one thing nor another. There is
Clapham, for instance; stuck-up houses and
bits of gardens always trying to look like

country. How I should hate to live there; although your hero, Mr. Granville Sharp, does live there, and other people who are something like him ! "

How much she had seen ! Clapham, I knew, was near London. My father had a first cousin there, to whom one day we were to pay a visit.

" What is it in you, Bride Danescombe, that makes me like you, and say everything I ought and I ought not out to you ? You don't say much. And I am sure you don't always like what I say. But you know it is quite useless for me to seem somebody else, and make you like that somebody else, and then wake up and find it was not me."

I wanted to say how much I did like her. But I could say nothing.

" Now," she said, with a little mono-syllabic laugh—(she never laughed in peals, only with her lips and eyes, and that one

little quiet musical dropping of laughter)—
" I will show you my likeness. I have kept
it for you since the day you called Granville
Sharp a hero."

And from a corner of the seat she took a
little crocus bulb. It had a curious long
appendage to it like an ivory knitting-needle.
" I found it lying forgotten and forlorn in
a piece of turned-up ground," she said..
" It could not get at anything to root itself
in, in any natural, proper way, like other
crocuses ; and so it shot down this ugly
thing, feeling and feeling for something to
twist its roots about. *And at last it found
something.*"

" Oh, Amice, Amice," I said, feeling those
motherly wings fluttering all warm in my
heart once more, " you mean you found *me?*
—*Me!*"

And I knelt down and put my arms all
around her, and hid my head in her lap,
and began to cry.

"I do love you. We have liked you so long, Piers and I. But oh, indeed, you want more than me. What am I?"

"You are a good, dear little soul," she said; "as kind as old Leo or poor Chloe. And with a kind of soul and conscience which makes you, on the whole, better than Leo, especially as I have nothing to do with it."

And she gave me such a long kiss, and such a long, close hug—her whole heart seemed to come into mine.

And then, with her little short laugh again she gently pushed me away, as one puts down a little child.

"There! what would Granny say? She would call it a 'scene.' And Mrs. Danescombe? All your pretty feathers ruffled as if you had been out in a south-wester. Come in and preen yourself, and Chloe shall help you."

Then again, with that quick sympathetic interpretation—"Not Chloe? Well, then,

I will. But you may tell your little brother
Chloe is *not* a slave. There are no slaves in
England now. Your Mr. Granville Sharp
got that settled years ago, as you might have
known, if he is such a hero, and you such
lovers of blacks."

On our way in we met Madam Glanvil,
as she was usually called in Abbot's Weir.

I had never seen her before, except at
church, or in state in her coach. And now
she was in her ordinary attire, a plain, closely
fitting woollen dress (woven in the cottage
looms of Abbot's Weir), rather short, with
a hood, all grey—not Miss Loveday's grey,
dove-like, but prosaic, black-and-white grey.

A very fine, erect, manly old lady, pacing
through her fields and gardens in stout
leather boots, with her steward.

"Granny is like me," said Amice. "Since
my grandfather died, she has had to do for
both."

Described in colour, her whole effect was

steel-grey, as Loveday Benbow's was dove-
colour. Her eyes were steel-grey, with
clear, steely gleams, and also stormy, thun-
derous flashes.

She looked me all over, not, however, in
a way which made me conscious of clothes.
Then she nodded rather approvingly, and
then she said—

"Go in and get ready for dinner. You
have seven minutes. Do you think I can
wait for children?"

"She says whatever she likes, and no one
can answer her," said Amice. "She is deaf,
you know—so deaf that she never hears
anything but what she likes, so that it is
quite useless to be angry or to defend one's
self. But she likes you, I see from her nod.
Granny's nod is like Jupiter's, you know,
in the Homer; so don't be afraid."

The dinner was silent. And again, the
weight of the big rooms and the black footmen stepping as softly as my stepmother's

cat, and the plate, and the Nankin China, like our very best, which was never used —were a little oppressive to me.

After dinner Madam Glanvil settled herself to her nap in a great chair by the window, and told us to go and amuse ourselves. But before she spread the Bandana silk handkerchief over her face to keep off the flies (of which she spoke in language so strong, it sounded to me rather like swearing), she called me to her.

"Stand there in the light, Bridget Danescombe," she said, "and let me look at you."

There was something in her direct, imperious way which amused me; and not feeling under her sceptre, I stood fearless, looking up occasionally into her grey eyes, wondering what she would say or do next.

"That will do, child," she said, with her Jupiter nod. "You may go away and play. You are like your father, except bits of you

that I don't know—your eyes and eyebrows.
I suppose they are your mother's.   The
Danescombes are not a bad stock to come of,
as old a family as any in the county, only
on the wrong side generally as to politics,
when there *were* politics worth thinking or
fighting about; the older branch, but Par-
liamentarians; the younger branch managed
better, stuck to the king, and are in the
House of Peers.   And I hear your father is
following the family ways—Whig, or even
Jacobin, or one of those philanthropists
who are worse, always minding other
people's duties.   Don't flush and blush, child.
People cannot help what they inherit.   I
have no opinion of people who change their
family politics or religion; although it is a
pity for them, of course, if they happen to
be wrong.   Your father is a gentleman and
a Danescombe—Danescombe of Danescombe.
The pedigree is right enough.   One thing I
regret—he should not have gone into trade;

though, certainly, younger branches and
decayed branches sometimes must. It is
better than begging, or than that vile law.
I've seen enough of that—always leading
one on and then turning against one and
making charges for talking and writing.
Beggarly! and the king's service certainly
does not pay, or the Church, unless there is
a family living. However, that's no affair
of yours. You may come here whenever you
like, and Amice likes. Only don't flush and
blush, or throw yourself into raptures. And
if Amice lends you a horse, which she may,
to ride over the Down together, don't be
nervous and throw it down, as town children
are apt to do. And if you can help it, don't
be a philanthropist. I will have nothing to
do with philanthropists. You look a sensible little maid, but rather soft and melt-
ing—the kind of stuff those people are
made of. And being in the family it is
dangerous—infectious too. And remember,

I will have nothing to do with philanthropists. There, go and play, or ride, or anything you like."

And drawing the Bandana handkerchief over her face, she dismissed us.

"But," I said to Amice, when we were alone, "it is a little trying that your grandmother should be deaf just in that way. It makes one feel dishonest not to answer her, especially when she says things about other people. If my father is what she calls a philanthropist, I am sure the last thing he does is to mind other people's duties. The motto he gave me was, 'Other people's rights and our own duties.' Is it quite impossible to make your grandmother understand? at least about father?"

"Quite," said Amice. "And if she did hear that motto, she would not like him any better for that. She would think he meant it was his duty to look after people's rights and wrongs; and that is exactly what she objects to, as to the black people you are all so fond of. But I like the motto, Bride. Only it might lead one no one can tell where; at least *me*."

The nearer I came to Amice the deeper the mystery in her seemed. It was like wandering through a great northern pine-forest, in the twilight; glimpses here and glimmerings there, and everything seeming to lead into a new infinity.

What had the shadows been which had lain so deep in her early life that they had made the faith natural to her a Manichean dualism? that terrible faith always ready to spring on us from the darkness of sin and sorrow, that evil is co-eternal with good, and in might perhaps co-equal.

CHAPTER X.

A WHOLE ocean of new life and thought was opened to us through the advent of Madame la Marquise des Ormes, Claire, and Léontine. There was also an Abbé, madame's brother, who occasionally appeared, but preferred to live in a large seaport town about fifteen miles off. M. l'Abbé, like many of his countrymen, was not complimentary to his land of refuge. He said the most comprehensible thing to him in the character of the English was their passion for the sea. He could for himself see no way of living in such an island of "*brouillard*" and "*bourgeoisie*," except by keeping constantly in view the one means of escape from it.

Among the four we had brought before us four sufficiently characteristic phases of the France of our day.

Madame was Royalist to the core, with the chivalrous old French loyalty which the death of Louis XVI. and Marie Antoinette enkindled into a passion and exalted into a religion. Monarchy and martyrdom united had surrounded the son of Saint Louis with a halo so mystically interwoven of earthly and heavenly splendours, that to see prosaic fact through it would have passed the penetration of any mortal vision. In the later days of Louis XIV., and through the reign of Louis XV., her family had lived a good deal in retirement on their estates. The ladies of the race especially had not shared in the sins and splendours of that corrupt and corrupting court, but had lived in familiar and gracious intercourse with their peasantry, never contemplating the possibility of a state of things in which great ladies could do anything but reign and distribute alms, and peasants desire anything but rapturously to receive alms and serve.

That there could be any great fundamental wrong in the nature of things which made it the highest hope of the majority of labouring men to end life as dependent pensioners on the bounty of the minority never occurred to them. How could it have done so?

Such wrongs intertwined with the innermost fabric of society are, I suppose, seldom perceived from within, until the slow growth of abuse at last interferes with some elementary law of gravitation or cohesion, and the whole edifice crumbles into decay or crashes into revolution.

Besides, unfortunately, it is precisely those who would most gladly correct such abuses who naturally come least in contact with them. Their own virtues clear the region immediately around them, and if anxious and foreboding politicians talk of "Augean stables," they reply, incredulously, "Was ever stall cleaner swept than mine?"

Madame des Ormes from the first seemed to single out our family. She was sure there was French blood in our veins—the highest compliment she could pay; there was a peculiar curve of the eyebrow in my mother's picture and in me, never seen in pure English faces. It was true. My mother's grandfather had been one of the exiles in the Huguenot persecution. Ours was the only house in the town she volunteered to enter. My stepmother she considered a little "*bourgeoise,*" but my father's manners she approved. Some people's manners she said were too much for them. Like badly made dresses, you could never forget that they had them on; and some people were unfortunate enough to have no manners at all. In the last category she included Madam Glanvil, who was the only person I remember her speaking of with a little tinge of hauteur.

Her natural social level was that of the Countess of Abbot's Weir. And I well remember the glory reflected on Madame and Claire, and even on Léontine, when the Countess's coach stopped at Miss Felicity's door, and the Earl and Countess went up into Madame's apartment.

I never knew what happened at Court. Madame, with M. l'Abbé and Claire, had been invited there with all ceremony, and entertained with all state; and Claire told me Madam Glanvil had offered to have them driven home in the family coach. But her mother had declined. "She was only a poor *émigrée*," she had said to Madam Glanvil, "and must disuse herself from such pomps." To Claire she said that nothing was so intolerable as that etiquette of the province, or "the great airs of the little noblesse." And she would never go to Court again.

Nor was Madame altogether charitable to Amice. She pronounced her a little wild: Madame "liked wild creatures in the forest —they had a fine free grace of their own; but in the *salon* one never knew what they would do next." "In a word, the whole household was Insular." I am afraid to Claire, Madame said, with a little compassionate shrug, " in fact, *English.*"

Madam Glanvil, on the other hand, whose classifications were rather generic than specific, at once set down Madame la Marquise as frivolous and given up to vanities, M. l'Abbé as an ancient dandy, and Claire as a butterfly, and all three as, " in short, *French.*" The only person of sense and character among them, she considered, was Léontine; but then Léontine was a Protestant, and made bargains, and did her work, and came to church like any other Christian, "so that she was scarcely to be called a Frenchwoman." I tried often to bring my two groups of friends together, but in vain.

The inevitable result of contact was effervescence. Pressed closer, it would have been explosion, at least, on Madam Glanvil's side. So I had to desist.

Meantime, whatever else we learned or unlearned, the meaning . of many words expanded wonderfully through our intercourse.

French and English ceased to be the simple, plain definitions they had been. It was evident to us there were so many kinds of French. And to Claire, at least, it soon became evident that there were many kinds of English.

Then that word "*bourgeois*," how many puzzles it made for me ; and also how many it helped to explain, in endeavouring to

translate it to myself or to Claire! How
much of English and French social life and
politics lay wrapped up in it! Had we
absolutely no synonym for it?

I had heard Madam Glanvil use the
expression "*town's folk*" with something
of the same unflattering emphasis. But
then, with her, that meant not merely the
lack of a social distinction, but of country
habits. She would have used it with
little less depreciation for fashionable men
about town than for unfashionable men
and women in Abbot's Weir. It meant
people who could not ride, or hunt, or
tramp about ploughed fields; effeminate
creatures who carried umbrellas, and could
not brave a herd of cattle. It had indeed
to do in some measure with trade. Certainly trade was not to be accepted except
as a last resource, and people who contrived to get rich by trade were to be set
down.

But, there even, was no sharp impassable barrier between gentry and "town's folk." People of good family had (unfortunately, of course) to live in towns, and to go into business. Claire's father, on the contrary, under the *ancien régime*, would have had formally to resign his sword, and his cachet of nobility, before he could demean himself by trade.

In England there was, indeed, an aristocracy prouder, perhaps, than in France; but prouder because less fenced in. Pride had to hold firm the barriers law had left open. Titles which in the third generation ceased entirely, and a nobility continually recruited from the bench, the manufactory, and the counting-house, were, in a very different sense, sacred from the great old noblesse of France.

"*Middle classes*"—did that express the thought better? In some respects. But

it also expressed the difference. Middle;
that is, between the upper and lower. But
where the upper ended and the 'lower began, who could say? Especially as neither
upper, middle, nor lower, were stagnant
waters resting at their own level, but all
in a continual state of ebb and flow in and
through each other; so that, with all due
respect to the catechism, the "station to
which God has called us" is by no means
a fixed line, always perfectly easy to de-
termine in a society where nothing is stationary.

"Pleasant old barriers," Madame des
Ormes thought, "when people were not
always struggling upwards, but content
with each other, themselves, and their
station." There *were* "stations" in those
days; and people had "leisure."

"Pleasant, picturesque old barriers," my
father said, "except that, within them all
the time was gathering the flood which

swept all barriers away, and much soil, and much life, which no floods could restore."

Pleasant evenings they were, when Madame des Ormes and my father sat on each side of the great chimney in the Stone Parlour. Madame always preferred the Stone Parlour. She said to Claire, who told me, that the Oak Parlour was like a state-chamber without the court; and the great drawing-room like a mortuary chapel without the sanctuary, only entered once a year, and terribly *bourgeoise*. But the Stone Parlour was like France, like the hall of an old château where they met after the chase. There were the sporting-dogs, and the great logs flaming and crackling, and cheerful talk, and going in and out.

My father spoke French easily, and understood it perfectly, a rare accomplishment for Abbot's Weir in those days; and to Madame his manner had a deferential courtesy which she said always reminded her of the old Court.

Her dress I cannot so clearly recall; I suppose because it always seemed such a natural part of herself. But her manner charmed me inexpressibly. There was such vivacity and such suavity in it; such grace and such freedom. And then her whole person seemed an organ of speech. She spoke not only with her voice, or with her eyes, like Amice; but with every graceful bend of her throat, and turn of her arms. And as to her hands, their movements were like music. They made her conversation as sweet and as varied as singing.

She was, however, not without serious anxiety about my father. She thought him, like her poor brother the Abbé, too "*philosophe;*" and had not they proved in Paris to what that led? Many a fragment of their conversation used to drop into our minds, as I was playing with Claire or Piers by the window, or as we sat silent by the fire, and interested me more than anything we were doing.

They had many a debate over Arthur Young, the traveller, in the course of which all kinds of curious details of old French manners and customs used to come out.

And those debates were sure never to spoil any one's temper. Many sparks were struck, but there were no explosions.

There was a common ground of tender pity for human creatures in general; and a sense that the world, and even the Church, in every corner of it, even to that most unsearchable corner within ourselves, needs a great deal of setting right.

Mr. Young, she would admit, might draw but too truly gloomy pictures of famished men, driven in herds across the hills, unfed and unpaid, leaving their own fields untilled to render serfs' service to the seigneur.

"But, Mr. Danescombe—he should not have left out the other side—there are hard masters and hungry labourers in all societies. Or are you, perhaps, so fortunate as to have none? Are those parish apprentices you spoke of all exactly content, and well fed? Mr. Young should have come to Des Ormes; and you also, Mr. Danescombe. We would have entertained you with an hospitality, not quite, I hope, unworthy of your own. You should have seen how the services our peasants had to render us in harvest or vintage or even on the roads were made quite a fête to them. We killed our oxen and our fatlings, and spread tables for them on the terraces of the château; and we, the ladies of the Castle, waited on them ourselves, and the sons and daughters of the Castle danced with them afterwards on the greensward. It was Arcadian; the costume of the peasantry blending with the toilettes

of the old Court (each, of course, keeping
to their own), the prince hand in hand with
the peasant. Our peasants complain of our
preserving forests for the chase? They
were never so happy as when they accom-
panied us in the chase, and I assure you
many a fine head of game found its way
from the seigneur's pouch to the labourer's
pot au feu. They were afraid to complain,
perhaps, you think? Quite the contrary.
I see here nothing of the free speech there
was between our people and ourselves.
The quick wit of our countrymen and
countrywomen, moreover, I assure you,
could give us as good as we gave."

(I had heard Amice say much the same of
the negroes.)

"They say our noblesse did not care for
the poor. Mr. Danescombe, never believe
it. Did not our mother teach us to make
petticoats and jackets for the old women?
And did not we dress the young brides from

our own wardrobes with our own hands?
Did we not make dainties for our sick,
and tend them by the sick-beds? You
should have seen our Christmas fêtes and
distributions. The people adored us. So
completely of the past as all that is, I may
say it now without vanity. They said no
garments wore, and no dainties tasted, like
those which came from our hands. Ah,
Mr. Danescombe, they make me forget the
Sermon on the Mount, those false accusers.
But in those days, believe me, there were
little secrets of that kind between us and
the good God, which, if the poor deluded
people forget, perhaps He will not. You
think we were an exceptional family. My
mother was perhaps an exceptional woman.
Her piety had been learned at Port Royal,
and some of our friends did sometimes
accuse it of being ' *tant soit peu Janséniste.*'
One of our estates was not far from Port
Royal des Champs. As children, we were

sometimes taken to see the ruins. My mother could explain them : the church which they filled with corn for the poor, the gardens and fallen cells made sacred by their prayers, made doubly sacred by their charity; and she would never leave those poor upturned graves without praying in memory of the holy souls of those who had lain there. As a child, I never quite knew whether, because by some inexplicable mischance they had missed the way of salvation and needed our prayers, or because we needed theirs. It was difficult. They were so saintly, so heroic, and yet condemned by those who should have known. Ah! Mr. Danescombe, sometimes a sad thought comes to me about our France. I wonder whether it can be possible, what our poor Léontine says, whether indeed we have driven away our heroes and saints, who could have rescued us ; and so have nothing left to our country but the martyrs, who can only die for us. These, you know, the good God, and the malicious foe, suffer not to fail in any age or communion. The tradition of those good men and women of Port Royal lingered long among the poor of the district. And we called our little daughter herself after one of them, Claire—from the friend of St. Francis, founder of the poor Claires— and Angélique after the Mère Angélique."

"It was a beautiful and tender tribute, Madame," my father said. "May Mademoiselle be worthy of both her patronesses."

"I do not say there were no evils that deserved chastisement, and needed correction," she would say. "God knows there were many. Our Great Monarch had been too much like a god, for a mortal man, though a son of St. Louis, safely to endure. There are traditions of Versailles we would willingly blot out. But we were changing all that. *We!* Mr. Danescombe, the poor noblesse whom your Whigs abuse, and whom our Jacobins have guillotined. Was it not we, alas! who commenced the Revolution? Did not M. de Noailles (M. le Marquis) propose equal taxation, the purchase from our order of certain feudal rights, and the absolute abolition of others, such as the *corvées*, or any compulsory service without compensation? And Mirabeau, and M. de Lafayette, mistaken as some of us may have thought them, were these men of the *bourgeoisie* or of the *canaille?* We had true instincts. We felt the tide must turn, was turning, and that we must lead it. And did we not try? We, and even our king?"

"You did try nobly, madame," my father said, sorrowfully, "at last."

"Ah, I know; it was too late. The stream was a flood. The tide was a deluge. But how could we tell? What could we do? It was, indeed, too late."

"Ah! Madame," my father said very gently, "I am afraid all reforms are too late which wait until the tide turns. All reforms which save from revolution must be not with, but *against the stream.* God grant we find this out in time. God grant England may not silence her heroes, and only be left her martyrs!"

But little Claire! Madame des Ormes, charming and sweet as she was always, remained a foreigner, an exile, with all her sweet easy grace, a little apart, on an elevation which we never. forgot, and I am not sure that she did.

But Claire was our own from very early days, our very own, with a difference, a fascinating difference of nature, of tradition, of ideas, of tastes, which made her always as fresh and interesting as a new story.

If Amice lifted me outside our home, not without a shock, so as to see that in a new light, Claire lifted us outside Abbot's Weir, and even England, and that without any shock. She saw everything and every person through such a sunny medium, and made the world so delightfully larger.

For one thing, she learned English, which her mother never attempted, and Léontine and M. l'Abbé never achieved further than as a means of commercial intercourse with the "barbarous people" who had, they confessed, received them "with no little kindness." She learned it carefully, thoroughly, only to the end deliciously blending her own idioms with ours, and giving to our English a clear staccato definiteness and delicacy which *pointed* it, as often she pointed my work, with the last finish of her accurate fingers.

And she taught Piers and me, in return, her clear, graceful French, enjoying our amusement with her mistakes, and never laughing at ours.

Claire was not exactly a child, according to our English ideas. She had no shyness, or awkwardness; she seemed to have been born with that gracious tact, and that ready *savoir faire* which made the wheels of every day's life run smoothly. Where we were self-conscious, possessed by self, she was self-possessed, possessing herself, and all her faculties.

It was her natural tendency to agree with people, and please them if possible; to find out their angles to avoid them; just as in our Teutonic natures there is often a natural tendency *not* to agree with people, and to find out their angles to rub against them. Hers was the graciousness of a true aristocracy, not instilled by maxim, but infused by the life of centuries. Stiffened into a maxim, it might have read, " *Yield; because it is our right to command.*" Through all the courtesy there was a touch of courtly dignity which made half its charm.

It was a sunny atmosphere that Claire lived in, a positive sunshine, like that of her own land of purple vintages and golden harvests; she actually saw things softened, illumined, with all possible lights brought out, and the shadows glowing with reflections of the light that dwelt within herself; whilst many of us see things at best through a grey, clear, defining, unillumining daylight, and pride ourselves in consequence on our truthfulness; as if sunshine were not as true as mere daylight. If Amice was like a Northern forest, full of glades and mysteries, Claire was like her own sunny land of vintage and harvests, and valleys that stand so thick with corn that they laugh and sing.

To make every-day life as pleasant as we can to every one around us may not be the very highest aim, but it is a good golden background for the severer work of life to be relieved upon. And it was on that golden ground Claire's world was painted.

Brave she was by instinct, and by chivalry of race, and ready to make her little person a shield against the world for those she loved or pitied, as she proved that memorable afternoon when she kissed me with the foolscap on.

But the joys of the fight were not at all comprehensible to her. Her delight was to make us all at peace with one another, and pleased with one another, and also with ourselves.

When she came into your house, she always found out something pleasant in it you had scarcely noticed before. If your windows looked south, there was nothing so pleasant as a sunny aspect; if due north, there was nothing like looking out from the cool shadow into the sunlight.

She taught us first to see how beautiful our quaint old town was, in its green hollow of the hills. She had especial delight in our wild flowers. The banks of the three ancient roads which wound from it up the hills, worn deep by the rains and tread of centuries, were, she said, each one a hanging garden of delights, from spring to winter. She and Piers and I used to go on endless expeditions laden with baskets, which in spring were filled with masses of primroses, violets, or blue hyacinths. These, of course, we knew and loved of old; but Claire had a liberality in her love of flowers beyond ours. Everything came well to her; things we had called weeds and rubbish, she contrived to make lovely nose-gays of; ragged robins, meadow-sweet, the starry hemlock, "twelve o'clocks," fox-gloves, woodruffe, blue corn-flowers. She made her mother's little apartment gay all the summer through, and when flowers failed she brought in leaves. Leaves were her speciality, she said, bramble leaves above all. She said the flowers were her English china, better than all the old majolica and Sèvres in the château, and the autumn leaves were her English bijouterie and bric-à-brac, richer than all the old bronzes, and ormolu, with their metallic crimsons, and bronze, and gold. And "in shape," she said, "flowers were nothing to leaves." " The good God," she thought, " having left out the colours and perfumes, had all the more beauty to spare for the design."

How choice and fair she made that little room of her mother's !

In the corner was a little, low, narrow bed, like a couch ; but Léontine had draped it with white muslin, always fresh, and contrived a coverlid out of some antique brocade, so that it looked like a canopied throne.

Then there was a little table, with a mirror behind it, and upon it a few relics, such as a jewelled snuff-box, with a portrait of a grandmother, powdered and frizzed, and one or two toilet ornaments. And in the window a common deal table, draped with muslin and frills, and always set with those rich masses of flowers, or leaves, in common white earthenware dishes, but looking as natural and at home as if they were growing on their own green banks. In a corner, a little table like an altar with a crimson antependium, and a delicately-carved, pathetic ivory crucifix on it; and a richly-bound prayer-book. On the walls were four or five miniatures grouped, and one larger head, often tenderly garlanded, of the king, Louis XVI.

We had nutting and blackberrying expeditions, Piers and Claire, and Dick Fyford and I, Claire declaring that no fruit in the garden was equal to blackberries; and many an opportunity was afforded to Piers of risking his life by gathering nuts and berries from impossible places up precipices and over rivers.

Our old abbey buildings, also, were great bonds of union between us.

These, Claire said, were as much hers as ours, being built by the monks, who belonged to all Christendom, when there was one Christendom, long ago. And she made the old arches and towers live to us, by telling us of an abbey close to her father's château, where real living nuns had been cloistered, where the lamp was always burning night and day in the church before the altar, and a sister kneeling before it, until the Revolution had quenched the lamp, and scattered the sisters, and turned the convent into a factory, and the church into a granary.

I suppose Claire would not have been a great reformer of wrongs; although she certainly would not consciously have inflicted any. She would scarcely have

pulled of her own will against the stream.
Side by side with any one on whom that
strain of energy devolved, she could lighten
the strain inconceivably by delicately indi-
cating how to avoid all avoidable collisions,
by keeping rowers and steersmen awake to
every counter-current and every possible
favouring breeze, above all, by keeping alive
in the hearts of the toiling crew, that
generous candour, open to every palliation
and every excuse for opponents, which is not
a little hard to maintain when the stream
against which they pull is the injustice
and selfishness of angry human beings.

As a sufferer of wrong, no one could be
sweeter than she was. Her hardest epithet
for those who had murdered her father, and
driven them all houseless and destitute
from their fair, bright country home, was
" deluded." Or if any severer denunciations ever passed her lips, they were always
levelled at an impersonal " *On*," which had

deluded every one. "Our poor, dear, deluded people," she would say, "they (' *on* ') persuaded them that they would find gold mines in our châteaux, that they would be Rentiers, and all their starving children live like princesses, without impoverishing us. I am sure they never meant to ruin us. How could they, with all mamma and papa had done for them all their lives, and grandmamma before? We loved them, these poor peasants, and surely they had loved us. They had danced us on their shoulders, and sung us songs, and laughed with delight when I lisped in imitation. I was their own in a way much as my mother's. And all at once they (*on*) came from Paris, and told them a quantity of falsehoods about the cruelties of the noblesse; perhaps also some true things, but certainly not what *we* had done. And those poor peasants went mad. And one night Léontine came in the middle of the

night, and drew me out of bed, and huddled
on anything she could find, and took me by
the little back door, where my mother was
waiting, through the wood, up the hill, to a
cabin, our woodman's hut. And there we
looked down and saw the dear old château
illuminated more brightly than for any of
our fêtes, but for the last time; flames
breaking out of every window, and those
poor, mad people shouting and dancing
round it, where they used to dance with us,
or wait for alms. They did not steal our
things. They burnt them, Léontine said.
And all because of what some wicked nobles
had done somewhere else to other people.
Was it not strange? Léontine said it was
because of things further off even than that.
She said things more precious than ormolu
and ebony had been thrown into the flames
in old times; men and women, men and
women of God! — her forefathers, she
meant,—the Huguenots. She said it was

God 'avenging His elect' at last. But *we* did not burn the people, nor hurt them, nor any one that we could help. And it seems a very strange kind of justice that my father, who was good to every one, should suffer because some one else's grandfather was cruel to people we never saw."

Poor little Claire! "*Solidarité*" was a word that did not exist in her French. And yet in other ways she understood well that nations are not mere conglomerations of independent atoms, but that there is a deep and terrible reality in the words "national life."

Léontine had her own interpretation of events, to which she steadily adhered. She was the only one among them to which the history of the Revolution did not seem an unintelligible chaos. " Generation after generation, Monsieur," she said to my father, " our poor France has driven away her heroes, those who could and would have saved us. It was not only that they hunted

the Protestants away.   It was the *strongest*
and *bravest* of all the Protestants they
hunted away. The gentle and timid and
helpless and womanly remained. The *men*,
the soldiers of the faith, the heroes, fled or
escaped, to you, to Holland, to Prussia. *Our*
strength and courage went to strengthen
you in Holland, England, and Prussia.
And so when the flood came, there were
none strong enough to stem it.   Even ladies
and gentlemen of Port Royal, Catholics
of the truest, spoke too much truth for
France, and they were trodden down. Generation after generation our poor France has
driven away her heroes, and silenced her
prophets, and now she has none but her
martyrs left.   But those, monsieur, believe
me, of the best. All our great ladies and
lords can suffer cheerfully, nobly, piously,
like apostles.   There is blood in France as
pure and noble as any in the world.   But
alas, it seems only to flow for the scaffold."

CHAPTER XI.

VERY soon after my first day with Amice Glanvil at Court, it was decreed that Piers's path and mine were to separate; that he was thenceforth to attend Mr. Rabbidge's boys' school, whilst I was to continue with Miss Felicity, with the understanding that three afternoons a week were to be spent with Miss Loveday, learning embroidery, fine needle-work, dress-making, and millinery in general, as far as Miss Loveday's exquisitely neat fingers and her very subdued tastes could instruct me.

It was a terrible day to me that first morning when Piers and I had to go our different ways to school.

He had a longer walk than mine, and had to start first.

He was full of glee. The last remnants of childish attire had been laid aside. There was in those days at Abbot's Weir no intermediate boys' costume. Piers sallied forth, fully equipped in a miniature edition of my father's "coat, hosen, and hat."

His very shoes had a manly tramp in them, as he marched down the street. And I stood alone watching at the old arched door, feeling terribly feeble, "female," and forlorn.

At the corner he had the grace to halt and turn, and give me a protective masculine wave of the hand, before he disappeared, so glad and free in his sensible, tight garments, made of things that would not tear, made so as to be convenient for climbing and racing, and everything I delighted in, and in general with a view to being as little obtrusive as possible; while mine seemed expressly constructed with a view to being obstructions in the way of everything it was best worth while to do, and filling up all the leisure spaces of one's life with making and mending them.

He had good reason to be glad; and for him I was proud and glad too. I would not have had him go a day longer with me for all it cost me.

To him it was a beginning, and through him for me also. But to me it was an ending also: so many things that are beginnings to brothers are endings to sisters.

He was to go on and out in so many ways —out into the world of boys and of men, out into the world of Greek and Latin, and all kinds of wisdom, ancient and modern— whilst I was to go no further than round and round Miss Felicity's history and mythology lessons, the geographical lists of countries, provinces and capitals, and the first rules of arithmetic, my only progress being out of "round hand," businesslike and legible, into " small hand, " angular, ladylike, and indefinite.

In my double relation to Piers I felt smitten. As his sister, I was never more to be his constant, hourly companion; as his " little mother," I could watch over him and protect him no more, except as a helpless hen-mother a brood of ducklings. He was launched into an element where I could not follow him; he must make his own way, meet his own temptations, encounter his own dangers, fight his own battles, whilst I could only cluck and flutter my wings on the shore.

And he liked it, of course; he delighted in it, felt a generous trust that I delighted in for his sake, and had no idea, should never have any idea, I determined, that when he was quite out of sight, I went into the Stone Parlour, and seizing the kitten, rushed up with her to the inmost recess of the old nursery, which was now my bedroom, and seating myself on the little cot that had been his, where I used to say my prayers beside him, and had felt like his little mother, cried bitterly, and sobbingly told pussy that now I had no one to take care of but her, " no one in the world ! "

The old church bell striking the school hour broke in on my lamentations. I symbolically anointed my head, and literally washed my face, crossed the market-place, and got into the school before the chimes had finished ; so that no one, I flattered myself, would see I thought it anything but a step onward in life, to have a brother at Mr. Rabbidge's.

But all the morning the tears kept very near the brim, and I felt Amice Glanvil's searching, wistful eyes on me.

At the end of the morning school, when we were left alone, as we often were, whilst she took the dainty little repast prepared for her dinner, she came up to me and grasped

both my hands with one of her abrupt,
passionate movements.

"Bride, I cannot be sorry for you," she
said. "I have tried. But it is of no use.
Next to being a man one's self, there can
be nothing better than to see one's brother
beginning to be on the way to be a man.
Think of what they can do! Think of what
he is going to learn to be, he and Dick
Fyford, and all of them. They are gone to
learn to be soldiers, to fight for England,
and sailors to man great ships for England;
and doctors, to cure people's diseases, and
lawyers to set people's wrongs right. (For
that is what I think lawyers are for, though
Granny says they are only to puzzle right
and wrong together so cleverly that no one
can find the way through without paying
toll to them.) And masters to employ
men; or writers of books to teach men.
How can you be anything for a moment
but glad that Piers is beginning?"

For she knew quite well I was not very glad.

"I shall be very glad to-morrow, Amice," I said.

"Then be glad to-day," she replied. " I have no patience with people who keep turning their faces the wrong way, and sighing and crying because we must leave things behind. Of course we are always leaving things behind. Look the other way and see what is before you, Bride Danescombe."

"I do not mind leaving things behind, Amice," I said, thinking her a little hard. "It is being left behind that is hard to bear."

"Then *don't* be left behind," she replied, with her rare little laugh. "Go on! I mean to go on, although I am only a girl. But then, of course, I have no brother, so I have to do for both. But if I had a brother, —a brave little brother like Piers—wouldn't we set some things right, together!"

"But I cannot go on, Amice," I said. "You know I have come to an end of Miss Felicity's lessons. And there is nothing to do but to go round again, and to sit still and sew."

"Sitting still and sewing *is* dull," she said, emphatically. "Happily for me Chloe does all that." Then, suddenly, her face flushed as with a new thought, and she added, "Do you know, Bride, I think I will ask Granny to let me learn sewing with you. One never knows what one may have to do. And in learning of Miss Loveday one learns so many things more than she knows she is teaching."

That was a bright prospect for me—afternoons with Amice and Miss Loveday; and I left the room greatly cheered.

But in the afternoon little Claire had made some excuse of a message to our house, and we crossed the market-place back to Miss Felicity's together.

She said nothing; but as she put her dear
little hands in mine, I knew well what she
meant. She wanted me to feel I had some
one to take care of still. And in the evening, between Amice's bravery and Claire's
soothing, I felt almost as bright as Piers
himself when he swung into the passage,
and his joyous voice rang through the
house, calling for me.

There was a button to sew on and a rent
to mend in those clothes which I had
envied as so imperishable. And there was
a history, brief but vivid, of the encounter
with a bully of a big boy, which had occa-
sioned the damage.

Piers had begun his battle of life with
wrestlings literal enough. He did not tell
me the name of his adversary, nor could I
gather quite clearly the issue of the encounter, except what might be inferred from
the explanatory statement that "he could
not help it, he could not see any fellow,

whatever his size, throw stones at old black Cato, and call him names, and not try to stop it, and if the big fellow were to try it again, he must do the same."

He had, moreover, a suspicious mark on his eyebrow, which, with all his anxiety to conceal it, and all my bathings, grew deeper in tint, so that Piers had to select retired places, lest my stepmother's vigilant eyes should detect that he had begun boy life so pugnaciously.

It was plain that there would be points enough at which my brother's life and mine would meet, and that he would need his little mother at many extremes yet.

Apparently, the "big fellow" did try it again, for Piers came back a few days afterwards with a peculiar twinkle in his eyes, and with a scar on his cheek.

" *He* did not give it me," was all he vouchsafed in explanation, " it was only a corner of a stone I came against in falling.

But he was under, and I don't think he will try it again."

"Other people's rights and our own duties?" I ventured to ask.

But Piers would explain no further.

"It was a mean thing, in his opinion, to brag of things out of school before girls."

The force of the contrasts was strong on him.

Dick Fyford, however, told me enough to show that Piers had won his spurs.

Claire and I were decidedly proud of Piers's black eye. It consoled us for being girls and being left behind, to find him so unmistakably a boy.

But all our small public opinion was by no means unanimous on the subject. My stepmother "must beg that for the future, if Piers could not keep out of quarrels, he would quarrel in a gentlemanly way, with gentlemanly boys, and not get his face disfigured in a manner which made it unfit for

ladies to sit at meals with him; and, above
all, not in his new coat. She wondered
Mr. Danescombe did not take the matter
more seriously. But it was so difficult to
persuade him to take anything about the
children seriously."

My father merely said—

"My dear, it is impossible not to envy a
little the sanguine Quixotism of these young
people. Piers," he added, "if your black
eye would begin to set the whole world
and all its wrongs right, it would be a very
well-invested black eye; and no doubt you
are of opinion it will. But remember you
have only two eyes, and only one new coat,
and for our sakes, please take proportionate
care of each."

Piers and my stepmother were both
silenced, neither seeing clearly where the
little sarcasm fitted best.

But Miss Loveday was profoundly serious
on the subject.

"My dear Piers," she said, in her gentlest voice, falling, as usual with her in agitated moments, into the "plain" Quaker mode of speech, "thee will never win the true battles in that way. The weapons of the true warfare are not fists."

"But boys have not any others, Miss Loveday," he said.

"It is written, 'Love your enemies,'" said Miss Loveday, with tears in her eyes; "Do good to them that hate you."

"But I have no enemies," replied Piers. "As to loving people who hurt other people who are helpless, I cannot. And as to doing them good, I think it is the best way of doing them good to stop their doing harm. I might have hated him if we could not have fought it out; but now there is no need to think of it any more."

Miss Loveday shook her head.

"Pride can forgive an injury it has

avenged," she said. "Besides, we are told what to do if we are smitten."

Piers made no reply; in the art of verbal self-defence he was not strong. Besides, Miss Loveday was a woman, and deaf; and to defend oneself against a woman in the vehement form argument is apt to appear to take with deaf people seemed to him, I believe, unchivalrous. But he said afterwards to me—

"It says nowhere, Bride, that we are to do nothing but be patient if *other people* are smitten on the cheek. And if the Sermon on the Mount means that, it must be meant for men, not for boys. Grown men have the Assizes and the Parliament, and all that kind of thing to stop other people from doing wrong; but we have nothing except our fists. Besides, there is the Old Testament. David and all of them often had to fight."

"Claire and I don't think you at

all wrong," I said, "nor, I think, does father."

But this did not console Piers. I think he was more ashamed of our admiration than of Miss Loveday's remonstrance.

"It *is* hard to have such a fuss about nothing, only because I was so unlucky as to get hit where it would be seen. Boys are always getting hit, of course."

In Ulphilas' translation of the Scriptures for the Goths, we are told that the translator left out the Books of Kings, thinking his Goths too likely to draw such encouragement as Piers did from the warlike proceedings therein recorded.

But Piers had plunged into the primitive age of lynch-law and "vigilance committees," with which the world is always renewing its boyhood for young human creatures and young nations.

Homer seemed to him an imperishable picture of life; only he could never make

out how the Greeks could both scold and
fight. The scolding, he thought, was the
natural share of those who could not fight ;
and the talking, of those who could not
work, or *make.*

Criticism he considered the natural province of women, or of men who have nothing to do. It was not till later that he
learned how some talking is making, and
some words are battles.

The streams of our lives seemed running
very far apart. For as Piers's life went
forth more and more into the din and
tumult, mine withdrew more and more into
retirement.

So much farther apart are boyhood and
girlhood, than womanhood and manhood,
the parting and distribution necessary to
the deeper meeting and uniting.

Even our amusements separated. Claire
and I pursued our strawberry, and flower
and blackberry gatherings, and nuttings,

our gardenings, and rambles alone, whilst Piers and Dick Fyford were shouting over cricket and football.

It was chiefly in making and mending that our lives seemed still linked.

For ministries in the form of mending there was no lack of opportunity. And Piers, now promoted to a real carpenter's bench and perilous workman's tools, constructed many a basket and box, and even chair and table, for Claire and me.

Amice, he always continued to maintain, was "almost as good as a boy;" besides, she had the glory of three additional years; and with her (his self-banishment from Court having been tacitly annulled in consideration of Granville Sharp's achievements) he had many a daring gallop, not to say steeplechase, over the downs and moorlands.

But it was always the flowers which Claire loved that he contrived to remember, and to pour out now and then in a careless, casual way from his pockets, when he returned from his expeditions, and to empower me, if I liked, to carry over the way.

Meantime, we sewed, and Loveday listened, like Joan of Arc to her "voices," and talked to us. That longing for the liberation of the negro slaves which she had inherited from her Quaker ancestry, and which had been as a patriotic passion to her lonely life, could not but come out in those long quiet afternoons. At first she hesitated to speak of it before Amice. But one day, when she had broken off in some story of wrong, Amice rose, and coming close to her, said, in those low clear tones Loveday always heard so well—

"Do not stop. You cannot tell me worse than I know. When I was a child, I heard the cries from the punishment house; I saw the spiked collars, and the scars. You cannot tell me worse than I fear. Tell me, if you can, anything to give me hope."

And Loveday told us the story of the struggle, so that the far-off fields of Pennsylvania and New England, where John Woolman and Anthony Benazet toiled for emancipation until not one Quaker held a slave, grew to us a land of sacred romance.

Dear to us also was the story of the poor bruised and half-blinded slave, Jonathan Strong, left to starve by his master, how he was nursed, and fed, and tended, and clothed by Granville Sharp and his brother the surgeon; and then how out of that movement of natural pity, obeyed, grew the whole noble immortal work of Granville Sharp's life; how, alone, against the stream of lawyers and judges, and against the law itself embodied in an iniquitous decision, and confirmed by the opinion of Blackstone, he turned the stream, and brought round lawyers and judges, and at last the very law itself, constraining Lord Mansfield to demand the broad issue which he had so long evaded, and to pronounce the liberating words, that whenever a slave touches English soil he is free, thus virtually pronouncing slavery itself a wrong, and laying the axe at the root of the tree which from that moment began unperceived to totter to its fall.

So we sat and sewed and listened afar off to the echoes of many warfares, until, under Miss Loveday's influence, sewing itself became ennobled to me, and seemed an essential part of the warfare.

" For in all wars," she said, "the battles are but the crises of the campaign, the tests of strength long trained and long tried. People are victorious by virtue of what they were before the battle. It is not only the men who wield the weapons that fight, but the men who bring the meat and bread, the men who till and plough, and sow the corn,

and herd the cattle, and," she added, with
a growing intensity in her voice, " the
women who bake, and milk, and churn, and
sew, and bind up the wounds."

Men's work : tilling, herding, ploughing,
and fighting.

Women's work : cooking, sewing, and
nursing; that is, making raw material of all
kinds, material, mental and moral, corn,
axioms, principles, into bread for daily use
and lint to bind up actual wounds.

Claire and I grew quite content with
our feminine lot. But Amice said, " some
women had to take their share in the
actual fighting, she believed."

" Queens," I conceded.

" All women have to be a kind of queens,"
she said, " when there are no men in the
family. There is no Salic law which screens
orphaned or widowed women from taking
their place on the throne, or their part in
the battle."

And sometimes she said to Miss Loveday, "It is the waiting that is so trying. If it were all real working, I would not mind a bit what the work was. It is the waiting and doing nothing for any one that eats into one's heart like rust."

"Waiting need not be doing nothing," Loveday said. "I have had a good deal of it, and I have not found it so."

"Waiting may be waiting on God," she added very softly, "and I think there is little work as good as that."

And as we looked at her patient face, so pale and worn, and yet so often radiant from within, we understood something of what she meant.

END OF VOL I.

VIRTUE AND CO., PRINTERS, CITY ROAD, LONDON.

www.ingramcontent.com/pod-product-compliance
Lightning Source LLC
Chambersburg PA
CBHW020844020726
47497CB00005B/1246